A LOST MINE
NAMED
SALVATION

A LOST MINE NAMED SALVATION

NELSON NYE

THORNDIKE
CHIVERS

This Large Print edition is published by Thorndike Press®, Waterville, Maine USA and by BBC Audiobooks, Ltd, Bath, England.

Published in 2003 in the U.S. by arrangement with Golden West Literary Agency.

Published in 2003 in the U.K. by arrangement with Golden West.

U.S. Hardcover 0-7862-5940-X (Western)
U.K. Hardcover 0-7540-7747-0 (Chivers Large Print)
U.K. Softcover 0-7540-7748-9 (Camden Large Print)

The text of this Large Print edition is unabridged. Other aspects of the book may vary from the original edition.

Set in 16 pt. Plantin by Ramona Watson.

Printed in the United States on permanent paper.

British Library Cataloguing-in-Publication Data available

Library of Congress Cataloging-in-Publication Data

Nye, Nelson C. (Nelson Coral), 1907–
    A lost mine named Salvation / Nelson Nye.
     p. cm.
    ISBN 0-7862-5940-X (lg. print : hc : alk. paper)
    1. Prospecting — Fiction.   2. Gold mines and mining — Fiction.   I. Title.
    PS3527.Y33L62 2003
    813'.54—dc22
                                 2003058236

A LOST MINE
NAMED
SALVATION

I

Oberbit Johnston came by his handle from the bullet-shaped gouge torn from the top of a sunbaked and leathery outward leaning right ear. He had been so marked for a much longer time than he cared to remember; it had nothing to do with the petulant scowl that scrinched up the eyes in his dissatisfied face.

If the truth must be known, not a little of this present testy condition could be traced to the three day bender undertaken to celebrate his recent return to the so-called blessings of civilization.

Still, it wasn't his hung over miseries or the emptied pockets he'd found on awakening that got up his dander so much as it was the nagging conclusion which had camped on his shirttail all the way back from ten weeks at Twin Buttes. All the good ground was gone. He'd come into this world forty years too late!

He'd taken this figure from considerable travel. No single-blanket jackass prospector had climbed more slopes or crossed more goddamn burning sand in these past twelve years than Oberbit Johnston, and you could put in your eye all he had to show for it. If hard luck were doughnuts he had piled up enough to start a dang bake shop!

They had called this burg too tough to die but any blind fool could see it was on its last gasp. It was the mines that had made it and every hole on the mesa was half filled with water, all the ore faces cut off and no pumps that they'd tried could lower it more than a handful of inches. His jaundiced stare counted vacated quarters of fifteen businesses folded or moved.

He couldn't think why the hell he'd come back. There was nothing here for him — not even a hope. The knowledge of his presence was enough to send folks into hiding like the heelflies were after them. He hadn't the chance of a snowball in Death Valley of finding another grubstake around Tombstone, or anywhere else he had ever been heard of. He doubted he could even raise the price of a drink.

All the wasted years rose up to mock him, all the miles he had covered trying to find him a strike. He hadn't always been treated like a leper in this country; he could remember when these pinch-faced galoots had sung a different song in his presence, crowding around with their tongues hanging out, ready to crawl just to stand in his shadow! He had never guessed then he would be in this fix.

Oh, he'd seen soon enough he would never get anywhere punching other men's cattle. A man in this world had to be his own boss if he didn't want to wind up swamping saloons. But it was the early bird that got the big worms — he'd been born too late and no two ways about it.

Greener than grass he'd been that first trip. Not knowing no different he'd supposed all a man had to do was get over the ground and — with both eyes open — he was bound to stumble onto some kind of paystreak; the irony was that he sure enough had. He'd uncovered the Silver King, richer than Croesus, and — seven feet tall — had stupidly unloaded it for five thousand dollars counted down on a bar.

Then he'd found the Bull Weevil, picked up a few partners to get things moving, and had been frozen out by some stock skulduggery and a lack of ready cash. The Bull Weevil, after he was out of it, had poured twelve solid millions into the pockets of his partners. And here he was without even a pair of nickels he could rub together.

He had thought for a spell that any dang chump who could stumble on two could sure as hell's hinges come up with another. Wasn't three the magic number?

Oberbit snorted. If it was, the law of averages had someway ceased to function. He had pretty near been over every square inch of ground in five hundred miles — some of them inches two and three times. Sure he'd found traces of color. Over in California, a place called Galler's Wash, he'd scooped up a brimming hatful of nuggets. It had raised up his spirits for the next couple years, but he couldn't find a vein or even the ledge they'd come off of. He'd been clean through the Panamints, had searched Furnace Creek, and hadn't once since so much as made day wages.

It was enough to cramp rats.

But he wasn't licked yet! Not if he could slip old Tallow Eye loose of the past week's feed bill piling up at that livery. Somewhere, someplace between here and starvation, even the worst of luck was bound eventually to change. And who could say this wasn't the day?

Tossing aside his whittle stick, folding his knife, Oberbit got to his feet with a groan. Feller must have rocks in his head to contemplate getting out into that sun with no better reason than he had. But a man sure tired of communing with himself and nothing he had hit on held out any promise of bettering his lot.

Putting the best face he could on un-likely prospects, he got off the warped planks of the Oriental's stoop and struck out boldly for a look at his mule.

The stage from points east rattled in on the wings of a boiled-up dust just as he was nearing the Wells Fargo station. Time he came abreast of the building some fat-ass dude was helping a woman from the coach's open door. Oberbit, astonished, paused to stare and gape.

Passengers for Tombstone in these sorry times were sufficiently unusual to com-mand a second look, but it wasn't the yellow-shoed fat dude in the dusty opera cape and derby that Oberbit's startled gaze was concerned with.

All his attention was centered on the woman, scarcely more than a girl not yet out of her teens to judge by her shape and flushed, perspiring face. A pair of thor-oughly cool eyes looked out of that face, inspecting Johnston briefly as she came to the ground, reclaiming her arm from the grip of the dude's hand.

She was dark, with an olive cast to her

11

features which no amount of sun appeared likely to impair. A dusty lavender dress held her closely at waist and breast. Her small hat with a half veil and plume topped gloss-black hair dropping in a long fall behind a proud-held head; her face, like a cameo, was exquisitely exact, full red lips imparting just a suggestion of the arrogance that too often traveled with inherited wealth or breeding.

In a graceful turn she stepped aside with the fat man to make room for a third disembarking pilgrim, a bony looking fellow with a rust-colored head and a high flat face that looked as blank as a board. The driver tossed down their bags, jumped off the wheel and, jerking a whiskered nod at the girl, strode off with a near-empty canvas sack in the direction of the door to the Wells Fargo office. "Grub in the station," he called over his shoulder.

Oberbit, indulging his curiosity, heard the skinny passenger grumble at the dude, saw the fat man shrug as the girl turned away. Tubby sure as hell hadn't fathered anything like her, Johnston thought, as the corpulent dude followed her into the station. So what was she doing getting off a stage with him? — and at Tombstone, of all places?

The other ranny, that skinny cuss in range clothes, was headed now in long strides for the Oriental's batwings. Oberbit had no difficulty finding a peg for him: he was stamped with all the hallmarks of somebody's hired gun. Were the three of them together or just coach companions? Was the girl the fat man's wife?

It was certainly no skin off *his* nose whatever their connection. But Oberbit, moving along again, found something mighty queer and peculiar in three people getting off the same stage at Tombstone. He couldn't think what would fetch *any*one to this place. Unless — remembering the rusty-faced gunfighter — they were on a still hunt for some hole to hide out at.

He swung west on Fremont, sighted the OK Corral and came out of his absorption with a curse for wasted motion. The Lexington Livery was back the other way, and he wished Jock Crabtree were back there running it instead of Moses Kelly, who had no more heart than a goddamn barkeep. With Kelly all transactions were strictly on the barrelhead.

The old walloper sniffed when Johnston slouched through the barn's open doors. "Don't waste my time or your breath," he yapped from a packing case seat against a dim wall. "That mule stays right here until you work out his board bill."

Oberbit swallowed his pride with a sigh. "When you want I should start?"

"First thing you hev to learn in this business is not to put off till tomorrow any chore that could better be tackled right now. Horses crap. It has to be moved. There's the shovel and yonder's the fork. You'll find a barrow outside the back door."

You might have thought from Oberbit's look the old man had spoken in some foreign lingo. Kelly said, "I don't wonder you haven't turned up no more ore. Takes work to produce anything that's worth hevin'." With a disgusted look he said, "I want them stalls swamped. If you ain't up to it, get the hell out and I'll do it myself."

Oberbit, scowling, gingerly hefted the shovel, then set it aside to go after the barrow. He trundled it like he was afraid it might bite him, set it down by the shovel to get out a red neckerchief and mop off his face.

Kelly watched with curled lip.

Oberbit put the shovel in the barrow. He went drag-footed across to the ladder to fetch back the fork. The old man said, "I'm about to wear out just settin' here

14

watchin'. What time do you reckon you'll git to them stalls?"

Johnston, scowling, dropped the fork in the barrow. "Does it make any difference to the goddamn turds?"

"Might make some to you. Better shove a little umph in it if you aim to go off with that mule this side of Christmas."

Oberbit, irascibly, grabbed up the barrow's handles and started for a stall.

Three hours later, a little more experienced and somewhat more flushed, he was still hard at it with a couple of stalls yet to go. Bushed, he paused to rest his aching back, taking time out to wonder — not seeing Kelly — where the old coot had got to. Probably stretched out in the loft taking a snooze!

Nursing his bitter reflections and trying to make up his mind whether to go on with it or quit, the scrape of a boot and voice sounds abruptly twisted his head in a look toward the entrance. The rusty-faced man from the stage stood in the doorhole grumbling at somebody outside the range of Oberbit's view.

More from curiosity than any desire to be helpful, he put down his shovel and stepped from the stall. "Lookin' for somethin'?"

"Got any horses for sale?"

"We've got horses," Johnston answered, "but you'll have to talk to the boss."

"Where's he at?"

"I dunno."

Before the rusty-faced hombre could comment on this the fat dude appeared in his opera cloak and derby. "What'd you find out, Sammy?"

Sammy said, "Nothin'."

"The boss has stepped out," Oberbit told him. "If you're figurin' to buy horses you'll have to see him. Name's Kelly."

The dude took a squint at his watch. "When'll this Kelly be back?"

"He might be up in the loft. I'll take a look."

But he wasn't. Coming back down the ladder Oberbit said, "If you don't want to wait you might try Biff Haines at the Pioneer Livery, or Dexter's place over on Allen."

The dude, swapping glances with the rusty-faced Sammy, said, "Where's the OK Corral?"

"Next block down. Other side of the street. But they've nothing to sell. Gone out of business."

The dude put his head alongside of Sammy's, muttering something Johnston

16

didn't catch. Then he looked at his watch again. "You know where we could find a feller named Johnston — Oberbit Johnston?"

Oberbit wondered if his leg was being pulled. "You won't get no horses from him," he said sourly.

"Understand he's a prospector. Been all over." When Johnston didn't answer the dude said, "He's in town, ain't he?"

Oberbit took a harder look at the pair, the uncomfortable thought running through his mind that some of these tight-fisted pinch-pennies around here might have put his accounts in the hands of a collector. That rusty-faced Sammy looked like a bad actor.

"Well — speak up, man," the dude said impatiently.

Oberbit eyed him through half shut lids. "What were you figurin' to see him about?"

"That's between him and me," the fat man said gruffly.

Oberbit, scowling, said, "Mebbe you better keep it that way," and turned back toward his barrow. But as he reached for the shovel a new voice, tangled in footsteps, said, "Dan, have you seen that man Johnston?"

It was the girl who had got off the stage with this pair. She was looking at the fat man when Oberbit said impulsively, "I'm Johnston, ma'am."

II

Green eyes opened wide as her head came around. "*Oberbit* Johnston?" She couldn't seem to believe it.

Fatuously grinning he pointed to his ear.

"But . . ." The girl peered dubiously. "I'm looking for the Johnston that found the Bull Weevil Mine."

"That's me!" chortled Oberbit, thumping his chest. "And the Silver King, too!"

"But I thought . . . You don't seem *old* enough. The man I'm trying to reach has been *all over* — a real desert rat."

"I been around." Johnston, throwing back his shoulders, chuckled. "From the Sierry Madres clean through Death Valley — and, if I do say it, that's gettin' over some ground! Ain't another galoot this end of the cactus been over more country in the last twelve years. If it's a guide you folks're —"

"Gee Hossifat! You goin' to stand there gabbin' all the rest the day?"

The livery's proprietor stepped in from the back with a look on his puss that would have withered an oak post, and Oberbit — not in the best of his tempers — departed, jaws clamped and red necked, into a stall where he proceeded to kick up a nauseous dust.

His boss, turning to the others, dredged up a smile. "Excuse me, gents an' lady, but the kinda hired help a feller gits these days you gotta keep doggin' their tracks every minute."

Rubbing together his big-knuckled fists, he put on his business face, wrinkling his mouth up to say more agreeably, "Moses Kelly — hay, grain an' horses. Somethin' I kin do for you?"

While the fat dude was getting himself primed to talk the girl asked the liveryman, "Is that truly the Oberbit Johnston who staked out the Bull Weevil?"

Kelly, noticeably shook up, took out time enough to slanch a glance stallward before wheeling back with a put-upon grimace. "That's him, all right — a walkin' warning of the evils of alcohol. No good to himself or anybody else. S'pose you're wonderin' why I put up with him. I kin tell you it ain't easy," the liveryman proclaimed with another hard look through the quiver of dust. "A man's Christian duty can become an awful burden — but you didn't come around to talk about that."

The dude spoke up to say, "We're looking for horses. Ones that'll get us there and still have some go in them. Don't show us no renters. We're fixed to pay cash."

"You've come to the right place." Kelly beamed, perking up. "If you'll step through the back door here . . ."

"I'll leave the horses up to you," the girl told the dude. "While you are taking care of it I will haff a conversation with —"

Across the dude's shoulder the liveryman yelped, "That scamp ain't free to farm out his time without someone settles this bill I got agin' him!"

Rusty Face gave the fellow a shove. "You worry right now about findin' us hosses."

But the fat man was quick to soothe Kelly's dignity. "We decide to latch onto him I'll pick up his tab."

Back in the cavernous quiet of his stable the black-haired beauty with the haughty Spanish features was making herself agreeable. The green eyes were bright with an excitable interest, the red lips curved like a cupid's bow about the husky cadence of words as delectable as processed honey.

"You are the first real — how you say? *célebre?* — I haff ever been so near to. In

20

my own contree, you onderstand, ladies of important blood is never talking weeth gentlemans like thees. Impossible! Even one so famous as you!"

She warmed him with the twist of a smile. "How is it you are clean these place? In my contree people make song of you — your courage, your cleverness, the fabulous wealth you haff found in the desert."

The green eyes glowed. Behind the yellow blouse she had on, twin bulges, swelling, rose and subsided like a wild pound of surf across glistening sand. Lost in his own rough palm, the feel of the timid hand she put out loosed a tumult in Oberbit that near left him dizzy.

She said, leaning toward him, "You are wonder about me — but, of course!" The teasing eyes searched his face. "Why, you ask, ees Micaela Mariquita Peralta y Moro — who come all the ways up here from Guadalajara — so eenterest in me? So!" She grinned. "I weel tell you."

And looked quickly around. "Someone we need who onderstan' thees contree."

Johnston, enveloped in a smell of crushed lilacs, hung on her words as though they were tenterhooks. Her voice fell away to a breathless whisper. "Who can help us to locate a mine that ees lost." Her head with its raven-black hair jerked a nod. "For three hondred year it ees gone — *desparecer.*"

The green pools of her eyes were large enough to drown in; yet Oberbit, invited, was plainly headed for dry land. She drew back as though affronted.

"You do not belief?"

"Lost mine!" Oberbit's lip curled. He might not know the first thing about females, but talk about mines and you were up against a gaffer who had skinned all his molars on the sharp barbs of experience. "Lost mines in this country come seven for a quarter — why, there's one behind every rock if you're going to swaller that kind of foolishness! Every dang chump an' his uncle has hunted clean on back to Cabeza de Vaca!" He blew through his cheeks a sneer vast with scorn. "You ever heard of anybody *findin'* one?"

She pushed out her chin. "I weel find thees one! For three hondred year —"

"Sure, sure," Johnston jeered, "it's been the talk of your family and everyone else that ever heard of your outfit. You're wastin' your time — I been all through them sunblasted hills. There ain't no Peralta mine an', if you want my notion, there never was!"

Her mouth was a white-rimmed gash of crimson across the look of a face gone stiff with resentment. "My father —"

Oberbit, peering down his nose at her, made a rude noise. For two cents, he reckoned, she would fly right into him, but he only snorted as one would at a fool. "If he believed that stuff, your father got taken in just like the rest of 'em by the kinda loose talk all these old coots make book by. Jacob Waltz," he said, sneering, "was never lost in his life."

The girl's lip trembled. "I haff a map —"

"You an' about six thousan' other nuts! Gettin' so the only people you can sell 'em to —"

"I didn't *buy* it!" she cried at him fiercely. "It's been in my family for —"

"Three hondred years," he said so aggravatingly complacent it looked a toss-up whether she would swear at him. She astonished him by grinning. He looked so taken aback she laughed.

He didn't like being laughed at, even by a filly as handsome as she was. If there'd been a hound handy he'd have kicked it for sure.

She pulled herself together. "Do you want the job or don't you?"

He was about to tell her what she could

do with it when he recollected the plight of his mule, and some other pertinently factual matters. He sleeved sweat from his cheeks and had another good look at her. "What's in it for me?"

Green eyes stared unreadably. "What do you want?"

He had chased enough rainbows over the years to want every cent he was able to squeeze out of it. He said, considering her craftily, "Two hundred a month."

She sucked in her breath. "Ees — ees that your best offer?"

"Rock bottom." Johnston nodded.

She said with an obvious regret, "We cannot pay it."

Oberbit scowled. "How you goin' to get an outfit together?"

"It weel take about all we can spare, I am afraid. Getting thees far along cost more than we had expected." She explained that when her father, a rancher, had died last winter it turned out he'd been living beyond his means. They'd had to liquidate everything to settle his debts. This had left her in such reduced circumstance that the only hope she had left lay in finding the mine.

"How's this fat dude fit into the picture?"

"Dan McCready?" She looked surprised. "He was Father's lawyer. He come along to look after me."

Oberbit snorted. "What are you payin' that rusty-faced jigger?"

"I do not know. Dan engaged him."

"To do what?"

"Dan seemed to theenk he'd be good to haff along."

Oberbit sniffed. "I'll work for what he's gettin'. But you'll have to get my mule outa hock."

"I haff a better idea." She looked at him earnestly. "Help us find the mine and you can haff half."

Oberbit grinned insufferably. "I still got my teeth an' most of my marbles. I guess not, lady. Half the Lost Dutchman is still half of noth—"

"I'm not talk about lost Dutchmens!" She skewered him with a glittering eye. "Thees mine no joke! *Mira!*" she cried with a hawk's glaring fierceness, one hand diving into the neck of her blouse. "Look for yourself!"

The hand reappeared, clutched about a small chunk of chalcedonic quartz which she pushed under his nose with a withering scorn.

It was blue — sky blue — worn smooth

and half polished through innumerable handlings. Never in his life had he seen anything like it, but no one had to tell him what the stuff was with those brassy oblong crystals so remindful of sylvanite. It had to be tellurium, the only element with which gold combines in nature.

III

"Lemme feel it," he growled.

Obviously amused, she flopped it into his held-out fist, not a bit put off by so gruff an attempt to hide his interest.

It was heavier than its size would have led one to suspect and, as Oberbit scowlingly studied the blue rock, the girl, smiling broadly, loosed a sound of satisfaction. "Now do you belief?"

Johnston scrinched up his face but could not hide his trembling hand. "Got any more of these?"

Micaela shook her head. "In Guadalajara, sí. *Poco mas* — but not here."

He hefted it again before handing it back. "Worth mebbe two bits," he said disparagingly. "Let's see the map."

The green eyes laughed. "I was not born yesterday."

She knew he was hooked and he knew that she knew it. Oberbit, staring, moved his shoulders in a shrug. "I been wrong before. Not much of that around — hard stuff to gauge. Feller in the Panamints, down by Lone Willow, south of Wingate's Pass, used every week to go by a big ledge of this color. Knocked off a few chips but never did nothin' about 'em. One day he run into Fred Carlisle at Joberg — Fred run the tests at the Red Dog. Got rightdown set up when he heard about this ledge but they never did learn if the ore was worth workin'. While they were jawin' a big storm come up and they never were able to find it again."

"I know what *thees* is worth." Mockery looked from the shine of her eyes. "Feefteen thousand dollars a ton — Dan had it assayed. I'll *find* it, too," she said with conviction. "Are you going to help?"

Oberbit, trying to look undecided, heard a nearing of voices and allowed he might as well tag along. He peered at her slanchways. "If your map's any good you don't need me, so why kick in for half?"

"Without your help it could take a lot longer. I want to be fair. We've got to haff someone who'll recognize points of reference," she said. "We don't want to waste time in the wrong stretch of contree."

"I'm not the only goat knows these hills."

A smile tugged the red lips. "But you are the only one *we* know about."

"I don't get it," he said.

"Dan had you looked up." Seeing how little this pleased him she said with a teasing lilt to her voice, "We know already you haff found two mines, that you haff much time spent in thees locality, that you haff no close friends and can keep a shut mouth. It was Dan's idea we should give you half — with so much at stake we can afford to be generous."

If they knew this much they must have found out, too, that he couldn't get a grubstake, was considered a poor risk. Of course her offer of a half could be the dude's idea of keeping him honest, but though he pushed this notion around he couldn't drum up much enthusiasm for it.

There didn't none of it seem to make a heap of sense but he was in no position to be examining too closely any deal packing rock that would run to fifteen thousand. Dudes, anyway, were notoriously fools.

"All right," he growled, "count me in. But I damn sure want this deal put on paper."

"Of course." She smiled; and when the fat man stepped in with his rusty-faced bravo leading half a dozen horses — three of which were saddled — she said, "Dan, give him the paper."

The derby-hatted McCready dug a legal looking envelope out of his suitcoat pocket and put it in Oberbit's hand with a nod. "Glad to have you with us."

While they were settling up with Moses Kelly for the horses Oberbit drew the enclosure from its covering and stepped outside to scan the typed contents where the light was still strong enough for him to be sure of what he was reading. Then, a bit disconcerted, he read it through again.

It was, so far as he could tell, a bona fide deed made out in his favor at Guadalajara ten days ago for a full half-interest in the Salvation Mine. Signed, sealed and delivered in person without stipulations of any kind.

He put it back in its envelope, folded it twice and then, on a hunch, strode back into the stable. He stopped in front of the girl and held the thing out. Micaela stared. "What ees the matter?" she said with her face turning stiff and her widening glance slanching a look at the fat man. The liveryman looked at him, too, then at Johnston.

Oberbit said, "Look it over."

She took out the enclosure, held it to catch what light was available. "I don't onderstand . . ."

"That your John Henry?"

She peered at him, baffled.

Oberbit said, "Did you *sign* it?"

She looked again. "But of course."

He hadn't really been in much doubt but it never hurt to make doubly certain. "All right," he grumbled, "you can sign it again. I want the fact witnessed."

The fat man said, "It's been witnessed. Notarized."

"Then it won't hurt to have it witnessed again. You got ink around, Kelly?"

The liveryman, much intrigued by all this, wheeled off toward a corner and came back with a pen and a grimy pot of ink. Micaela, somewhat snootily, proceeded to write her name once more. "Put the date alongside," Oberbit told her and, when this was done, held the paper out to Kelly. "You sign it, too," he said, "right underneath there, an' put the word *witness*."

Kelly read it first and astonishedly whistled. "What's she givin' you half of this mine for?"

"I don't think," said McCready, "we need to go into that. Your only function is to witness her signature."

The liveryman scowled, then eyed Oberbit craftily. "How much do I git for it?"

31

"How would you like a punch in the nose!"

Kelly, muttering, scratched his name and Johnston impatiently grabbed back his paper. Micaela said, "Take care of the board bill for Oberbit's mule, Dan."

"How much are we stuck for?" McCready asked, and the liveryman promptly hiked the price double, Johnston thoughtfully keeping his lip buttoned.

Then the fat dude, about to put away his wallet, said, "We'll be needing three pack saddles —"

"I'll pick 'em up," Oberbit said hastily, ignoring Kelly. He saw no reason if there had got to be charity why it should not begin at home. "I'll take care of it with the rest of our camp gear when I stop around to pick up supplies."

McCready looked at him in a kind of sharp way but fastened up his wallet without further comment. When they all got outside the rusty-faced gent, still in charge of the horses, came up and thrust the tangle of reins in Johnston's hands. "You can start in earnin' your keep right now."

"I got to go pick up my mule," Oberbit growled, not minded to do any work he didn't have to.

"Oh!" Micaela said, "you haven't met Sammy Darling. Sammy, this is —"

"I know who it is," Rusty Face said unpleasantly. "Horses is *his* job. I signed on to furnish protection."

"We've all got our chores," the McCready dude said in his patriarch's voice, the sonorous tones rolling over Oberbit's protest with a world of assurance. "A man who is hired could hardly be expected to assume the responsibilities of a full partner in this venture. We set out for the mine at midnight, Mr. Johnston — see that everything's in readiness. You may pick us up at the hotel, sir. Good evening."

IV

Oberbit, gaping as they started away, flung down the snarled reins. "Here — hold on! I sure as hell didn't figure to be chief cook an' —"

"And what, Mr. Johnston?" the fat man asked, head twisting to eye him across a hunched shoulder.

"Well" — Oberbit scowled — "I sure didn't figure to be no *flunky*."

McCready came around. "The responsibilities —"

"Never mind that. Let's get down to brass tacks!"

"Certainly. Somebody, obviously, has got to be in charge of things," the lawyer pointed out, not unreasonably. "Sammy's talent does not extend to putting together what we'll need for this trip, nor do I feel myself capable. Miss Peralta, convent-reared, could hardly undertake the direction or details of what seems likely to prove an arduous journey. One of the reasons I had for seeking you out — the thing, in fact, that recommended you most to me —

was your experience in such matters."

Examined in that light Oberbit did not appear to have been left much to complain of. Confused, he gulped a couple of times sort of sheepishly and began to feel himself over as though not convinced he was still in one piece.

He pawed at his face. "But I don't even know where the hell we are *headed!*"

The lawyer's mouth seemed to flex and draw in like the neck of a purse and the glittery slanch of his persuasive stare shoved a look at the girl before swiveling back to encompass her partner. "I am glad you reminded me. You know of a place called Pleasant Valley?"

Johnston peered as a man sometimes will who imagines his ears have played him some kind of trick. "N-north, you mean, of the Mogollon rim?"

It came out like the bleat of a frightened lamb.

McCready, if he noticed, gave the squeak in Oberbit's voice no attention. Solemnly nodding, "To the best of my belief," he said.

"Hell's afire! That's no place to hunt mines!"

Oberbit's perturbation looked too plain to be ignored but the fat man's assurance remained unshaken. "Nevertheless," he declared, "that will be your objective. You will lay in whatever supplies are needed for the trip, plus return, and . . . ah, ten days beyond."

He fished out his wallet, studying a moment while he chewed at his lip. Extracting a thin sheaf of bank notes he tendered them to the new chief of staff.

With eyes looking about to roll off his cheekbones, Johnston backed hurriedly out of their way.

"Jesus Christ, man," he said, "you tryin' to get us all *killed?*"

The fat man's stare looked him up and down. "I can't seem to discover . . . What's the matter with the place?"

"You can't get in — an' if you do you'll stay. Day or night every trail is watched!"

McCready and the girl took another look at each other. Micaela asked anxiously, "Is there some kind of plague or something?"

"You better know it! Sheep an' cattle — they got a blood feud goin'! The Tonto Basin war —"

"That's got nothing to do with us," McCready said, and Oberbit swore.

"It damn sure will if we go up there. You better give them shooters time to cool off," he told the lawyer earnestly. "Six plantin's they've had already up there an' that don't count the ones dropped in gulches! Every guy an' his uncle has been dragged into it — you can't stay neutral an' keep your hair!"

McCready smiled a thin smile. "We'll see," he said like he was speaking of weather, and took the girl's arm as he turned away. The rusty-faced Sammy, with a grunt, strode after them.

"Dudes!" Johnston snarled, throwing down his hat to peer expressively after the girl and her escort. He was minded to quit and take his mule and get out of this. He even put some thought on it, but ore worth fifteen thousand a ton wasn't easily put aside by a man with ten years of *borrasca* behind him. There might be other mines but he had lost the knack of turning up any.

He wasn't one to put much stock in the dazzling chimera of lost lodes either, but that piece of blue quartz Micaela had shown him — while it might have been picked up pretty near anywhere — was a powerful persuader. For ore like that, Johnston told himself, a man could put up with a heap of tomfoolery.

Yet he was far from sure he could honestly trust any part of this deal. So little about it appeared to have any relation to reality — save maybe that rusty-faced gun coddler, Darling. This half partnership business! And having that paper all fixed up for him that way! They must think he was ready for a string of spools!

Oberbit, glowering about him uneasily, had the disquieting notion he was someway being set up for a sucker. Sure it didn't make sense — there was nothing they could possibly get out of him but work. Just the same, he didn't like it.

To begin with, there probably wasn't any mine, but then where was the use in all these arrangements? Why outfit a trip into hostile country and risk being shot without they stood to profit enormously? The gold-backed currency clutched in his fist was real enough anyway.

He shoved it into his pants with a frustrated mutter. He had never fallen in with such a bunch of queer fish. That fat silver-tongued shyster with his come-hither eyes and outlandish getup; convent-bred Micaela with her snuggly looks and jiggly bulges; and that poker-faced Sammy Darling, hand always hovering not two inches from the worn-slick look of that bone-handled pistol.

A feller had to be plumb weak in the head to hitch up his wagon to that kind of outfit! Oberbit guessed he should be shot for the simples, but no matter how riled with suspicions he got he couldn't push that piece of blue quartz from his mind.

He stomped back through the stable to pick up his mule.

The liveryman, redding up the chores Oberbit had quit on, poked his turkey-necked head above a stall. "I like a man who remembers his friends."

Johnston, ignoring him, went through the back door. He spotted Tallow Eye in the farthest enclosure and turned back to growl, "Where's my hackamore an' White River saddle?"

"I'll fetch 'em," Kelly called. "Wait right there — I'll fetch yer mule, too."

Looked like the Johnston stock had come up.

Oberbit snorted. Any chump fool enough to believe this would swallow anything.

He climbed onto the top of the nearest pen, quite willing to wait for such unaccustomed service while pushing around again in his head the notion of putting far apart tracks between himself and those crackpot dudes. He dug out the bankroll he'd been given for supplies and was nearing two hundred in his count of the dollars when Kelly, eyes popping, came up with the mule.

For once the old walloper appeared to be speechless.

Oberbit, stuffing the bills in his pocket, got down off the poles and stepped into his saddle. In sardonic humor he tipped his hat. "Give my regards to all inquiring friends —"

"Hold on!" Kelly squeaked. "Whereabouts is this mine you've fallen heir to?"

"Hoo hoo!" Johnston laughed deep down in his chest. "I'll bet you'd give a pretty to know! Even give me this stable an' the shirt off your back —"

"Well . . . sure!" Moses Kelly piped up, mopping sweat. "We'll go pardners in it if you'll give me first crack at gettin' in on the ground —"

"How about settin' up the drinks to that?"

Kelly stared, looking stabbed, but the burgeoning prospect of getting rich quick was too much for him and with a jerk of the head he went scurrying off to dig up his snake juice.

Oberbit, chuckling to himself at the idea of putting one over on a skinflint reputed still to have his first nickel, reined old Tallow Eye on through the stable and out at the front where Kelly, overtaking him, handed up his jug.

Holding it up long enough to the diminishing light to make out that the contents had been considerably lowered, Oberbit, wrenching the cork from the neck of it, threw back his head and poured the rest of it into him.

He blew out his cheeks. "Whew-wee!" he sighed, handing down the emptied jug. "I just needed that. Well, keep your fly buttoned . . ." He picked up his reins.

"Damnation!" Kelly cried, grabbing Oberbit's leg. "You promised to tell me about that strike —"

"Ain't no strike. Far as I know there ain't even a mine except what you read of it on that paper. Discovered, they say, by one of the Peraltas. Been in the family three hundred years —"

"Never mind that," Kelly whined, beside himself. "Just tell me where it's at!"

"That's the whole point of it, why else would they have come lookin' for me? Damn thing's been lost. All they've got is some crazy old map." He shook off the hand.

"But you said —"

"I been engaged to outfit a hunt. That's about all I'm able to tell you — except," Johnston said with the twist of a grin, "where we'll be headin' ain't no place for weak hearts. We're goin' up into the Tonto country . . . case you want to send love to the Grahams an' the Tewksburys."

V

He could joke about it now but was all too aware of the unhappy possibilities lying in wait for any dang fool brash enough to go sticking his nose into Pleasant Valley. Them boys up there, from all he had heard, were meaner than gar soup thickened with tadpoles.

Thinking along these lines, with the bulge of that bankroll chafing his leg, Oberbit was so bothered — so mixed up in his mind from contrary wants — about the only good feeling he had left from that drink was the nagging compulsion to put another on top of it.

Deep down in his secretmost innermost innards he had long nursed the notion that if you ignored a thing persistently enough more often than not it would go away. This comforting philosophy did not seem to be doing too much for him now. The inescapable advent of Micaela Peralta and her piece of blue quartz had pushed him between a rock and a hard place.

He wanted plumb urgently to ride

straight away from this deal and forget her. Twice after leaving the Lexington Livery he jerked the mule around with this resolve firmly clutched, only to curse and turn back, the lost Salvation and what he might get out of it exerting a pull no amount of common sense nor prickles of dark forebodings could for long overcome.

At the general store he picked out a coil of rope and ordered his foodstuffs, laying out particular instructions with regard to their packing. Midway through this dissertation the proprietor, thoroughly familiar with the chancy aspects of involvement with Oberbit, demanded without any great amount of tact to be shown what he proposed to pay with. Lips skinned back like a cornered coyote's, Johnston whipped out McCready's roll and fanned the ends of the bills before the man's startled stare.

"I'm payin' with these, an' I'll pay when I get my stuff. If you want my business it better be ready inside half an hour!" Saying which he stalked out through a stupefied silence.

He still had tarps and pack saddles to get, some carbines and blankets and a few other oddments — and the pull of good whisky was hard to resist, but he wanted right then an opinion even more. An acquaintance at the Mountain Maid, he figured, might supply this.

Accordingly, he turned west down Allen, past Fourth and Third till he could see the gallows frame of the mine's abandoned hoist sticking starkly from blue and restless shadows off to the right. Tallow Eye snorted, perhaps from ill humor, as Oberbit kneed him between silent buildings in the direction of Hop Town.

Johnston, paying no attention to this protest, kicked him hard in the slats and forced him drag-footed through. With peeled eyes Oberbit scanned these backlots surroundings, finally chancing a highgrader's whistle as the reluctant mule cautiously approached the vicinity of the shaft.

The Mountain Maid Company had closed down the operation but had not yet decided to completely relinquish the machinery and other removable assets pending further investigation; they still hoped that pumps, if they could get the right kind, might resolve their dilemma. Pursuant to this they'd installed one of their shift bosses to act as watchman-caretaker.

At Johnston's second whistle this fellow came forth, a naked gun in his fist as he emerged from the obscurity of the hoist house, hard-staring. "Why the artillery?"

Oberbit hooted. "You fell out with them gambasinos or somethin'?"

"Oh, it's you!" the watchman snorted. "Well, for your information I don't deal with ore thieves. So if that's what you've come for you can turn right around."

"Don't get in a pet," Johnston said placatingly. "All I want's a bit of information. Be worth five bucks for your time an' bother if I weren't so goddamn scared I'd insult you."

The mining company's man said gruffly, "Insult me some more or git the hell outa here."

"Ten bucks?"

"I'll take it." With the bill examined and stashed in his pocket the watchman allowed, "Must be powerful important to fetch that kind of manna outa you. What's eatin' you, Johnston?"

"Didn't you hail from around Pleasant Valley?"

The man, staring hard, abruptly said rather curtly, "So?"

Oberbit shrugged. "Much minin' through there?"

"Not that I ever heard of. Some gopherin' mebbe like you get all around. That's ranchin' country an' a powerful good place to stay away from right now.

46

They got a war on up there, case nobody's told —"

"How about *lost* mines?"

"Don't tell me," the caretaker said with a snort, "you been bit by that bug! For Chrissake, Johnston, when you goin' to grow up?"

Oberbit scowled, but in the interest of information decided to let that pass. "Lot of Spaniards huntin' treasure through this stretch in the old days. I just —"

"Yeah. Them Peraltas!" The caretaker's lip curled. "With a Lost Dutchman hid behind every bush!"

Johnston pawed at his face. "Well," he growled, "thanks anyhow. It was just an idea . . ."

"About on a par with the rest of your notions," the company's man flung at him gratuitously. "If you're huntin' a place to waste more of your time why don't you go down around Ruby an' Oro Blanco — that country at least has got a showin' of color."

"I might just do that." Oberbit waved and, turning his mule on the proverbial dime, heeled that waggle-eared beast into motion.

He went back where he'd left McCready's ground-hitched horses, scooped up the reins and headed uptown to pick up the rest of the gear they'd be needing, including filled canteens — which put him in mind of the thirst he'd been nursing ever since testing that cactus brew of Kelly's. It was Oberbit's hope that with sufficient lubrication the future might perhaps appear a little less dire.

From much experience and canny haggling he managed to drive several thrifty bargains, through piecemeal dealings with folks who needed money. That none of these purchases were recent importations or tricked out with the latest frippery bothered him not at all. They were serviceable and, on the whole, probably as good as if not actually better than McCready could have assembled had he gone the rounds himself.

This also left Johnston with enough spare change to cut the rough edge of his apprehensions and cache away among the packs enough more of the same to ward off the more pronounced miseries of snake bite.

With all this finally put in order he left the whole outfit at the Pioneer Livery on Toughnut Street to be grained, hayed and watered while he stepped around to the Russ House Bar.

It must, by this time, have been well on

the way toward the zero hour. Among the out-of-work miners crowding the mahogany (from the collection of shanties just across the way) he saw a sprinkling of troopers in galluses and blues and a pair of cocky hands he knew from Fire House Engine Company Number One who heralded his arrival with uproarious shouts.

After the usual horseplay and insults one of these, with his face shoved against Oberbit's good ear, wanted to know in an overloud whisper if Ma Johnston's favorite black sheep son was about to open up another bonanza. Somehow this joshing — of which he'd had more than plenty since being hoodwinked out of his equity in the Bull Weevil — spread a glow of heightening color above Johnston's frayed and sun-faded collar.

"When I come back," he scowled — "from where I'm goin', I just *might* have somethin' that'll open your eyes — you an the rest of this dog-rotted town! We'll see then who has the last laugh!" And, grabbing up the two bottles the apron had brought him, he flung a handful of coins on the bar and stomped out.

VI

At McCready's insistence their first camp was pitched soon after daybreak in a clump of cottonwoods along the east bank of the San Pedro just a whoop and a holler below the old Mormon settlement of St. David. Had it been left to Oberbit they'd have pushed on to Benson and taken their rest where there was something to do besides pound one's ear, but the decision was taken out of his hands when the girl cast her vote with that lardy-assed dude.

It was the lawyer's contention that most forms of trouble stemmed from argumentative opinions, greed, envy, hate or money troubles, and that the surest route to peace and tranquillity was in remaining unseen. He proposed doing their sleeping though the heat of the day, staying off roads and avoiding all manner of inhabited places.

While willing to concede some precautions might well be in keeping with the nature of their endeavor, Oberbit thought it just a bit thick to implement vigilance to such an extent. "Hell, you might just as well resign from the human race!"

"Sometimes," McCready snippily replied, "that would seem to be the only sensible solution."

Oberbit, when he got back his wind, hauled up his jaw with a kind of snort. But though he looked his contempt he threw a double hitch about his urge to debate, having already learned you might as well argue with the shadow of death as attempt the last word with a scissorsbill of McCready's caliber.

Let him play Daniel Boone in his humbug cape and brown derby if he figured this was going to keep their whereabouts in question. He had a heap to learn about life in these hills, and Johnston reckoned with a sort of grim relish the day wasn't far off when some Graham or tough Tewksbury would be setting him straight.

The second night out, still following the river, found them skirting in the tender hours the star-hazed footslopes of the Rincon Mountains. They'd been making pretty fair progress despite the dude's repeated objections that the pace was too cruel for a girl's fragile strength. She didn't look too pooped to Oberbit and if the horses could take it he saw no reason to be slowing down for her.

"This here's Injun country," he told the fat dude and his rusty-faced shadow, "an' the sooner we git out of it the better I'll like it." He jerked his chin toward Micaela. "You want to see that black mane ridin' the point of some redskin's lance?"

McCready, showing a little green about the gills, drew in a startled breath and caught up his reins without further critical comment.

"I don't aim to stir up no thunder of hoof sound," Johnston told the two men, "but there's a chance our health might stay a lot healthier if you'd see that this packstring steps right along."

Sammy Darling said across a curled lip, "Ain't been no Injuns broke loose in two years," and spat from the side of his mouth.

It would have been hard to say whether the contempt he displayed was directed exclusively toward feathered marauders or intended to embrace Micaela's new partner. Oberbit, without going into the matter, observed somewhat dryly it was good to have along a gent who understood them.

They passed Cascabel on the chillier side of four o'clock and pushed on with brief rests toward Redington, which they skirted in first light, moving far enough beyond to decrease the likelihood of chance encounters, making camp against a bluff well removed from signs of travel.

The third night brought them in the vicinity of Hayden, where the San Pedro swung eastward and was consequently left behind. They were coming into mining country now. It was Oberbit's notion they should take the road that went through Superior. "It's a hell of a lot quicker," he said, "than plowin' through these mountains tryin' to lay out a trail of our own."

But McCready refused to extend his approval. "Too much chance of being seen on the road." The girl backed him up, and Johnston said, snarling, "For Chrissake! Who are we tryin' to hide out from?"

"It isn't a question of trying to hide," the fat man declaimed; "it's plain common sense. We're hunting a mine that could well be worth millions. It belongs to Miss Peralta and she doesn't want —"

"Half of it," Oberbit growled, "belongs to me!"

The lawyer pursed prissy lips. "I'm aware of your legal rights. I should think you would want to protect them."

"I can't see what usin' the road's got to do with it."

"The lost Salvation has never been recorded. Until we've filed claims and staked the ground all around it, how much do you think your half is worth?"

Having it put like that, Johnston reluctantly gave in. "We'll follow the Gila through Kearny to Kelvin and, about halfway to Florence, cut north through the desert around the Superstitions, goin' into them somewheres west of Tortilla Flat."

"Just so you keep us out of sight wherever possible. Four people with pack horses could cause a lot of speculation."

"Four people with pack horses," Oberbit said flatly, "ain't goin' to be that easy to hide. Grapevine's probably workin' overtime right now. Moses Kelly, for one — where you got these horses — has got a bump of curiosity bigger than Ripsey hill. I done what I could — told him I'd engaged to take you folks huntin', but he had him a look at that paper you give me before he put his John Henry on it."

McCready brushed this aside. "He has never heard of the Salvation Mine. Nor has anyone else, because it hasn't been worked for three hundred years. That stableman's got no idea of its whereabouts. It's not him that worries me. What I hope to avoid is having people see us going into those mountains."

"I can't guarantee that."

McCready's silence was enigmatic. He produced a cigar and snipped off the end with a tiny gold cutter on the end of a chain from a pocket of his flower-embroidered waistcoat. With the weed in his mouth he said genially, "Just put us into them," and waved him on.

Johnston didn't know why the picture of McCready with that cigar in his face should keep flopping around through his head like it did long after they'd made camp and he was bent above the fire throwing together a buckwheat breakfast, but something was sure as hell picking and poking and it wasn't a thing from which sweet dreams are fashioned.

They caught what rest they could after eating, but even out of the glare it was soon hot enough to fry eggs on the rocks.

Johnston quit fighting it and got up in the middle of the sticky afternoon, moving around refilling the canteens and, afterward, thus reminded of his thirst, taking a good belt from one of his hidden bottles before climbing through brush to have a look at their backtrail.

He wasn't honestly disappointed when the landscape proved to be as barren as expected. He wasn't, on the other hand, particularly relieved. The unpinpointable disquiet engendered by that last exchange with McCready still continued to nag and put him presently atop a rocky knob from which a larger expanse of passed-through country appeared reasonably visible across the low humps of roundabout hills.

Off yonder, above those empty flats, a dust devil churned like a drunken waterspout, suddenly dissolving as the wind leaked out of it. No other movement caught his eye, yet he stayed awhile to watch a bit longer, belatedly conscious of perhaps having said more than discretion warranted before stalking out of that Russ House Bar.

But he'd said things before in the grip of resentment more times than he could count these past few years and all it had ever fetched was a laugh. So why should anyone now put stock in the windy mouthings of a guy notoriously down on his luck? No one had bothered to follow him before. Not even the bastards who had put up his grubstakes.

Things were different, though, this time. Even if Kelly decided to keep his lip buttoned about the mine and that partnership, them bums around Tombstone would soon enough learn about the horses McCready had bought off him. And the things Oberbit had bought and paid cash for. Just that in itself would have made this trip different — more than enough to stir up talk.

And there was Weminuche Bill at the Mountain Maid. Ten bucks' worth of questions from Oberbit Johnston were not going to be forgotten if talk's widening ripples lapped against *his* boots.

It was a worrying thought in the light of McCready's remarks. It wasn't what he'd said but how he'd looked that kept jabbing Oberbit; and now a further worry cropped up.

Against the powdery haze of smoky heat lying blue in the sun dance against the far horizon, two tiny black smudges had begun to materialize.

Beneath a shading hand Johnston watched long enough to make sure these were riders. To make sure doubly certain he continued his vigil, hoping they'd turn out to be working cowhands going about their workaday chores, maybe riding a line if they weren't hunting cows.

But they came straight on, too far away to recognize details, but giving every impression of following a trail. The trail McCready and his party had left no longer than early this morning.

Johnston swore and scrambled down from his perch, swearing again in frustration and anger as he stared toward the camp. That dude was like to throw up a fit, but he had to be told and that was all there was to it.

There was no point in waiting. Dark was still more than three hours away and in that length of time those sign readers yonder would be practically on top of them. Already they looked bigger and clearer, but not clear enough to make out who they were.

Squaring his shoulders, Johnston strode into camp, shook McCready awake. "Pair of riders headed this way. Looks like they might be follerin' our tracks."

VII

The dude blinked and stared, after which he fished around to come up with a stump of gone-out cigar which he carefully rekindled before tucking it between the grab of his teeth; then he abruptly shoved up and peered at Oberbit again.

"What makes you sure they're interested in us?"

Oberbit, someway, felt a little let down to find McCready taking it so palpably in stride. "Mebbe you better have a look for yourself."

"Not my forte. Ever see them before?"

"Kinda far off to tell. Probably some of that Tombstone pack."

"Can you lose them?"

Oberbit considered. "Not this side of the Superstitions."

"How far off are they?"

"Couple hours, mebbe."

"Can we get into the mountains this side of dark?"

"Take some pushin'."

"Get at it, then — I'll wake up the

others. Sammy'll give you a hand."

Oberbit, grunting, took off to get up the horses and throw on their packs. He couldn't see much likelihood of getting into the mountains, even the nearby ones adjacent to Kearny, in time to hide tracks and get out of sight before the pursuit — if that's what it was — discovered their point of entrance.

There was about one chance in a cartload that what had seemed a brace of waddies hot on their trail might, in fact, have been nothing more substantial than the distortion of heat glimpsed through refracted light.

Such mirages were common enough around sand country, only most of the times the things a man stared at appeared upsidedown — inverted. The guys he had watched with horses between their legs hadn't been like that. The horses had been *under* them, ordinary looking as a pair of old boots. And one — that high-stepping thoroughbred — was like a mislaid memory the way his thoughts kept pecking at it. And just about as tantalizing, Oberbit reflected with a scowl of frustration.

It was a cinch he hadn't seen it recent or he'd have hit on what was bothering him, hooked it up with some rider or incident instead of scrabbling around in his head like old Aunt Hetty pawing around for her specs when they were still on her nose.

He pushed it out of his mind and had the horses about ready with all the gear packed in place by the time the bleached-eyed Sammy sauntered up to stand, chewing on a blade of grass, with thumbs hooked over his shell belt. Oberbit gave him a surly stare, waved a hand at the dude and climbed onto his mule.

He led off to the north a mile west of the road, putting down a trail through pear and cholla that here and yon was surprisingly brightened by the scarlet tips of wolf's candle or the flowering shapes of paloverde and ironwood. He made no attempt at this point to hide their sign, content to cover as much ground as possible while the terrain remained reasonably flat.

When the going began to roughen into low hogbacks and foothills, near Kearny some forty minutes later, he took several backward looks from naked outcrops along their spines without once sighting any evidence of pursuit. But the absence of riders or dust from their passage held little significance if they were up against codgers who belonged in this country.

Johnston now swung west, aiming toward a range of mountains that flanked the Superior road for miles. If they had any name he had never heard of it, but the highest peak — which was opposite Sonora — was called Mount Mineral and this, at the moment, was the goal he had in mind.

The country grew rougher as they wound their way through a jumble of footslopes and gulches, climbing steadily away from the desert floor. Scrub growth, brushily stunted by poor soil and made arid through too little moisture, scabrously thatched bare hummocks of granite while a plethora of rocks in divers shapes and sizes not only impeded them but made each horse-length of hard-won progress increasingly chancy.

The girl, paler now in the gathering gloom, was determined enough to keep her mouth shut but McCready, bruised, scratched and irritable after a couple of whacks across the face from low branches, wanted angrily to know if there wasn't a better way.

"That Superior road is better," Johnston grunted. "Wasn't my idea to git into these mountains."

The fat dude subsided, but after another long half hour of bucking this trail he called out again: "Think we've lost them?"

Oberbit, pausing to give the animals a breather, twisted around in his saddle. "At least we've slowed them down for a spell." He peered at Micaela. "We're about through the worst of it. Once we've rounded this peak we'll be back on the desert and can make better time. If they haven't quit they'll spend half of tomorrow gettin' through what we've covered in the last hour and a quarter. I ain't countin' on it, mind you, but I don't expect we're like to see any more of 'em."

They spent another hour getting back onto the desert and by that time the moon was up, a lopsided orange bucket of a moon that made the country spread out ahead of them look like something from Dante's Inferno. The occasional saguaro with uplifted arms stood sentinel like some anguished lost soul against a blue sea of sand that stretched into infinity.

The girl said at one point, wrinkling her nose, "Does anyone *live* in this awful place?"

"Gila monsters, horned toads, coyotes, jackrabbits an' more dang snakes than you would want to run into, includin' some ranchers an' a handful of Injuns. Pretty good country if you could git water into it."

He saw the girl shudder, and pushed on again.

After a while McCready called, "What time do you suppose we'll get into the Superstitions?"

"If we wait out the sun," Oberbit answered, "like enough not before this time tomorrow night. You could see 'em now if you knew what to look for. Straight ahead, mebbe seventeen miles —"

"If that's all the far it is," the fat dude began, "I should think we could be there by daybreak if we'd put a little steel into these —"

"You start badgerin' them *caballos*," growled Johnston, "an' we *will* have our work cut out. A galoot without a horse in these parts had better start makin' peace with his maker!"

"That's right," grunted Sammy, biting off a fresh chew. "He ain't got long if he's used up his water."

Prissy mouth sucked in at one corner, the lawyer shot him a frosty look but abandoned the subject without further comment. It was just about then that straight out of the blue Oberbit recollected the identity of that black he'd observed carrying one of that pair back yonder.

She was Molly McCarthy, Jack McCann's

mare from over at Galeyville, Curly Bill's Cherrycow hangout, a place that roared straight around the clock. The implications of her presence — if it was Molly — on their backtrail really shook him. McCann was a gambler and the mare had won every race she'd been put in.

The point, however, that most concerned Oberbit was how she came to be camped on his shirttail. Was McCann on her back or had he lent her to someone who thought it might be profitable to tail these dudes to wherever Johnston took them? Was her rider Curly Bill, called sometimes Graham and sometimes Brocius?

This thought was enough to put shivers in anyone, for in these past few years, Curly Bill had become the most notorious outlaw in the Territory's history. Every lesser crook in this end of the cactus was believed to owe some sort of allegiance to him. Sure, he was supposed to be dead according to Wyatt Earp, who claimed to have killed him out in the brush prior to his own departure from Tombstone, but Wyatt had claimed a number of things no one had ever been shown any proof for. And if Curly was on that black thoroughbred now there would be powder burned before this was through with.

Among the many other things laid at his door it was rumored Curly Bill and some of his outfit had wiped out a whole mule train of Mexican smugglers at Skeleton Canyon to get hold of their packs of minted silver. If he'd got wind of what Oberbit was up to, the end, while uncertain, was apt to be near.

Johnston could hardly think what to do. He guessed he had ought to tell the fat dude, give him some warning of what they were in for. Yet if it wasn't Curly Bill there'd be no point in getting his wind up. There was only the pair of them after all, and anyone else he and Sammy should be more than a match for — having been fore-warned. Yet he was pretty sure now that big black he had seen was Jack McCann's mare; and Curly Bill and McCann were held to be *buenos amigos* — thicker than cloves on a Christmas ham.

Johnston decided for the moment to keep his guess to himself. Then, recollecting the girl, he again changed his mind and in the end rode back and gave McCready the full benefit of his suspicions. Once more the dude surprised him. His bird-billed face tightened up and his eyes winnowed down to inquiring slits but it did not seem to put him much off his feed.

"You make sure there were only two of them?"

"I had 'em in sight for at least fifteen minutes. If there'd been any more they should've shown up by then."

"I would think so." McCready nodded. "Not much point in harassing Miss Peralta — we'll just keep it to ourselves, eh? I'll tip off Sammy. Looks like the three of us should be able to stand off anything they try."

Oberbit wasn't too sure of that, particularly if one of that pair happened to be Curly Bill, about as hardcased a gent as ever flipped a pistol. No one but a fool would figure to take that feller lightly.

"Better keep our eyes skinned."

"We'll do that, certainly. Might even be wise to post a guard when we're in camp. No sense taking unnecessary chances." The dude dropped back to tell his gunfighter.

Left alone with his thoughts Oberbit reckoned he might as well have saved his breath. About all he'd accomplished, so far as he could see, was to set himself up to cut his sleeping time in half. He didn't reckon playing sentry was any part of McCready's intention.

VIII

Not until they'd crossed the second pair of steel rails in the gray of morning's earliest light did Johnston begin to look about for a camp site, presently swinging down to throw off the packs in a brush-fringed barranca on Kings Ranch range. Due north a few miles, against sun-brightened spires of the legends-haunted Superstitions, starkly towered the fissured monolith known to hundreds of treasure hunting optimists as Weaver's Needle.

Oberbit, giving this a sour glance, got a small fire going and began rummaging into a pack for the tools and ingredients to whip up a meal. In country like this you had to eat what you fixed or throw it away. Nothing spoilable could withstand the fierce heat of the long afternoons and ice hereabouts was more precious than gold. Not that you could find any — it was hard enough to find water.

Which reminded him that most of the canteens were just about as empty as a profligate's pocket.

Micaela said, standing over him, "I do

not theenk I weel ever want to sit down again."

"You'll git used to it." Oberbit grunted. "Hide'll toughen up. First couple weeks is what takes it outa you. Try a dab of bacon grease."

He handed up the bucket. With a kind of gulp she looked as though he'd offered her a snake and went trotting off like the heelflies were after her. It *was* beginning to seem sort of rank.

He scooped a gob into the bottom of his skillet, sliced three spuds and reached for the jerky.

Picking up the coffeepot, he made the rounds of the canteens and, as sourly predicted, got nothing at all from Micaela's or McCready's. He emptied what little was left from Sammy Darling's, pieced out the pot with water from his own, which hadn't been lowered but scarcely an inch, dumped in a fistful of cracked java beans and set it over the fire's edge to simmer.

The dude called his name and he reluctantly lifted the skillet off the blaze to go find out what McCready wanted.

"Those rails we crossed," the lawyer said.

"Yeah? What about 'em?"

"Where do they go?"

"A good ways south of us they wind up at Mammoth — that first batch, I mean. The ones we just crossed hit off east to Superior an' Globe, then drop down through Safford to join the main line at Bowie." He stared, eyes sharpening. "If you mean do the steam cars go where we're headed . . ."

The fat man nodded. "That was what I had in mind."

"You can quit dreamin' then. They go west out of Phoenix. Nothin' gits into that country up there that don't go on four feet."

McCready heaved a disgruntled sigh.

"If it's them fellers back of us that's got your wind up, the chances are Curly Bill ain't one of 'em, an' nobody else is like to come within spittin' distance without we just plain lay off an' let 'em."

He went back to the fire to get on with his cooking, considerably less sure of what he'd said than he'd have liked to be. Letting out a sudden shout and waving both arms, he broke into a run; the mule, hauling his tongue from the java spun around and took off. Oberbit grabbed up the teetering pot, took a hard bitter look and slammed it back on the fire.

"Come an' get it!" he yelled, and the first one up was the rusty-faced pistolero.

Sammy shook his head when Johnston reached for the pot. "You don't think, by Gawd, I'm goin' to drink after no mule, do you?"

"If you figger to drink you ain't got much choice. I had to take your water to fill up the pot."

The gunfighter grinned. "That I know. But there was still quite a bit left in yours so we're even."

That night, some two thirsty hours after breaking camp, Oberbit, pointing into a saucer-like hollow, told the fat dude, "Yonder's Tortilla Flat. There're springs there — good water. We'd best fill everything we've got. There's a crick up above but it's probably gone dry."

The group pushed on and, having filled canteens and wet their whistles, stood around waiting while the horses were watered. "How far," the black-haired girl asked abruptly, "ees thees Tonto Basin from where we are now?"

"It ain't the distance but the ups an' downs they don't put on no maps that makes the horses' tongues hang out," Oberbit confided, pulling on his brush jacket against the increasing chill. "As the crow flies," he told her, "it's scarcely more

71

than twenty miles, but you better not figger on gettin' there tonight. Be crowdin' our luck to make it by —"

McCready, in his pontifical fashion, declared, "We're not going to 'make' it at all. We're not going there."

"Not —" Oberbit, staring with his dropped open mouth, yanked the slack from his jaw and in a swearing voice cried, "But, goddammit, you said —"

"Watch that language, Johnston! I'm quite aware of what you were told. In the legal profession it's a standard procedure." He smiled a bit dryly.

"But you can't get to Pleasant Valley without —"

"Pleasant Valley is not included in our itinerary. We deliberately misled you as a kind of insurance against the very contretemps now striving to catch up with us. In a word, against *pursuit*. Come, man! Did you suppose we were naïve enough to put ourselves so completely in your hands?"

In the turmoil of his confusion Oberbit wasn't catching more than fifty percent of those four dollar words. What did come through was the fact he'd been hoodwinked — plain lied to.

He was not a man to be jockeyed with impunity. Not after the soul-blighting experience he'd incurred with the Bull Weevil. But he had learned not to wear his heart on his sleeve. Insurance by misdirection was a kind of operation that was right up his alley. And so, dissembling his resentment behind a show of stupefied ignorance, he demanded to be told how he was expected to act as guide and uncover the lost Salvation when he didn't even know what destination they were bound for.

"A reasonable question merits a reasonable answer," McCready said smugly. "For the moment you can steer us toward a place called Sunflower. Do you know where it is?"

Oberbit knew, and was minded to say they could dang well steer themselves and to hell with them, only just about then he remembered that piece of blue rock Micaela had shown him, and decided it was a poor time to be venting his spleen. The lost Salvation maybe didn't exist except on that paper they'd drawn up for his benefit, but he and that girl hadn't come here for nothing. If they figured on packing this pack string with ore he would be a real chump to walk out on them now.

"I can find it," he growled, "if you're sure that's what you want me to do."

Micaela, with twin spots of red in her

cheeks, said, "I am ashame we haff deceive you. Now I am tell you the truth. The contree we look for is near thees place, maybe three hour away."

"The Mazatzals?" Oberbit was staring with his jaw dropped again.

"They're on the map," McCready said, and tapped his pocket. As if, Johnston thought, that proved anything. But he could not hide his excitement completely. Some of it got into his voice when he said, "Somebody else may have found it by now. . . ."

The dude shook his head. "I don't think that's too likely. I've had a man up there scouting around for investments. According to the information he sent that's all ranching country, both sides of the Verde. No hint of a mine past or present around there."

"Any sign of blue quartz?"

"That was one thing," McCready said, "I was careful not to inquire about."

IX

The only difference in direction brought about by the change in destination given him by McCready was that now their route lay more truly north. It did not promise faster progress. In this forbidding tangle of cliffs and gulches, towering peaks and rock-strewn canyons where half the time you couldn't even see out, one had little choice in the matter of direction. You went where you could and hoped to hell you didn't come up against a dead-end wall or get so turned around you lost your bearings completely.

Quite a number of folks had, going into these mountains. A lot more had come into them than ever got out. Sheriffs' posses had found the bones of a few, people known to have been hunting the elusive Lost Dutchman; two or three of the skulls had had bullet holes through them.

Johnston kept his eyes peeled. He'd no intention of leaving his skull, bullet pierced, to the ministrations of coyotes and buzzards, or falling prey to the confusions that had trapped other men.

The possibility of the pair he had seen being still on their trail he put out of his thoughts, devoting all his attention to the business in hand. He'd been through from this way a time or two before and figured to remember enough to insure carrying this trek to the same desired conclusion. Ignoring McCready's frequent pieces of advice, he pushed them doggedly along toward a morning's camp on a shelf high above a boulder-choked gully where, in the concealment and shade of straggly spruce and piñon, he elected the fat man to stand first watch.

Although McCready seemed inclined to argue, Oberbit, standing firmly on this course, picked out Sammy Darling to relieve the dude at ten. "I'll take the third trick," he told the rusty-faced pistolero. "Make sure you don't call me short of twelve thirty unless somethin' comes up you ain't able to handle."

It was a desolate spot, far removed from the interminable cacophony of inhabited places. In this kind of quiet a man could hear himself think and Johnston had a few thoughts to iron out before allowing himself to relax and fall asleep.

★ ★ ★

When the gunfighter roused him in the heat of late noon Oberbit told Sammy, "Git the rest of 'em up. We're goin' to move straightaway."

He didn't wait for an argument but, injuning up on the drowsing horses, began to throw on their packs like he couldn't hardly wait to get shed of this place.

When McCready grouched over to find out what was up, Johnston said succinctly, "The tricky part of this *pasear* is just up ahead an' I've no dang mind to tackle it in the dark." He handed around a few chunks of stringy jerky. "Stuff this in your mouths," he bade, "an' let's git started."

The fat man, keeping his thoughts to himself, studied Johnston inscrutably, stepping into his saddle without further talk. Micaela, sighing, also mounted, but Sammy Darling, a little less reticent than was his custom, wanted grumblingly to know what this daylight traveling was going to do to their schedule.

"Prob'ly put us into Sunflower," Oberbit said, "some three–four hours ahead of when you figured. Which might be a good thing, seein' as how it'll find the most of that burg still tucked between the sheets."

Sammy and the fat man exchanged cor-

77

rosive glances. Johnston, wooden-faced, banged a run-over boot heel against the mule's ribs. McCready and the girl swung in behind and Sammy, herding the packstring, stuffed fresh twist in his jaw while bringing up the rear.

If Oberbit was at all uncertain about which course to take when choice was offered, any doubts he felt were admirably concealed. The lawyer saw no signs of hesitation, no evidence of confusion. He and the girl now and again indulged in brief snatches of conversation, generally kept too low to be intelligible, but Johnston paid no attention to them anyway. Much as he could he seemed to be keeping the peak of Pine Mountain in sight dead ahead, otherwise taking whichever way looked easiest.

Micaela just before sunset told McCready she thought Johnston worried more about the condition of the horses than he did about them. The dude, merely grunting, remained absorbedly wrapped in his own considerations. Shortly thereafter, while he rested the animals, Oberbit passed around another ration of jerky — "Just to keep up your strength till we can git a square meal."

The fat man flashed him a bit of a grin. "I trust you're not thinking to bypass Sunflower?"

"*I* ain't," Oberbit inelegantly told him, "but it's lucky I'm not called to speak up fer you."

The lawyer said, staring, "And what are we expected to infer from that?"

"Slice it any way you like," the prospector said, and poked his gray mule toward Pine Mountain again.

Actually Oberbit had just been sort of running off at the mouth, a bad habit picked up from too much time spent alone in the years he'd been trying to turn up a bonanza. What he felt about McCready wasn't sortable like fish or collar buttons into the bins of personal opinion labeled people he didn't like. All he felt sure of about this fat dude was that something — maybe them four dollar words — didn't inspire quite the confidence the girl appeared to accord him.

He had a way about him — no getting around that. He was handsome enough to have his face in white stock on a whisky advertisement, persuasive enough to be a real drawing card. He looked the kind of a feller you might run for mayor, bluff, easy talking, hale and well met. While speaking he looked you straight in the mouth with all the weight of authority vested in a judge.

Yet for all these plus marks the man's eyes reminded Johnston of sheathed claws; he had the feel — if not the looks — of a softly purring cat. A gent with something McCready wanted could, if he proved tough enough, get to be standing on pretty thin ice. And any girl fool enough to let him manage her affairs was sure as hell asking to become a plucked chicken . . . without she had someone like Johnston to look out for her.

He wondered if this was why she'd had that paper drawn up so far in advance: to act as a kind of brake, perhaps, in restraint of her old man's legal beagle. She didn't look like no fool — dewy-eyed to be sure, and a sight too young to have had much experience; but she must have had some sort of hunch up her sleeve or they wouldn't have come by to look for *him*. It wasn't that slick-talking dude who'd engaged him but the girl herself, Micaela Peralta, who had seen his worth, dug down and handed him half her mine. It was she who had told the dude to give him that paper.

For her sake he guessed he'd string along awhile. He sure as cripes had nothing *better* to do. There was nothing around Tombstone he could raise a strike out of; and that map she had, if it had been in her family for three hundred years, just might turn out to be worth a real stake.

The next time she pushed forward to ride with him a spell he asked if she really knew anything about it, how her kin had come to have it.

"The mine? But, of course! All my life I hear of thees mine."

Away back somewhere in the passage of years a Spanish king had made one of her forebears a baron, Don Miguel Nemecio Silva de Peralta de la Cordoba, first Baron de Arizonac, and with this transaction had deeded him a tract of land which today, had it been provable in court, would have comprised nearly seven-tenths of the present Territory. Claims, indeed, had been instituted on behalf the Peraltas but so much time had gone by, with records lost or mislaid, that nothing substantial, apparently, could be done about it,

McCready, however, was still earnestly endeavoring to wrest something out of it for her. He had gathered, she said, certain maps, *cedulas* and *expedientes* by which he hoped to make her claim to the grant a matter of record. Though this in itself proved nothing, it could — at least by McCready's tell — set up a climate which could prove to be financially valuable.

Oberbit, scrinching his brows in perplexity, failed to see how, but Micaela seemed to take the big dude's word for gospel. For one thing, she said, a number of ranchers already had come forward and paid cash money for quitclaim deeds. A kind of prima facie evidence, McCready had told her, tending to uphold the legal stature of her contentions.

This meant nothing to Johnston, who had never mastered the intricacies of legal hocus-pocus. But his ears stood out in considerable astonishment when she told of a certain mines-owning mogul who was sufficiently impressed to be staking McCready to five hundred a month to help defray expenses while he continued his search for the missing records. Also, and prior to this, the Southern Pacific — if you could manage to believe a quarter of what she claimed — had paid them through a subsidiary called the Pacific Improvement Company the whopping sum of fifty thousand dollars for a right-of-way.

Regardless of what Oberbit thought of the shyster, it began to appear that in the world of high finance Dan McCready was nobody's fool. He wasn't talking their claims up to shop clerks or office boys.

"And did you know," she said earnestly, peering into his face, "Señor Barney, who now owns your Silver King, gave Dan five thousand dollars in exchange for a quitclaim signed by me?"

Speechless, Oberbit stared with his mouth open.

X

Fed to the gills with such impossible tales, Oberbit lifted the gray mule into a lope, opening up enough ground between them to give the whirl of his careening mind sufficient respite to settle back on its rockers. Given half a chance, it looked like that pair could talk a cow right out of her calf!

But, hogwash or not, the part that really unfurled his fury and put up his back like a cat in a hailstorm was that reference to Barney and his Silver King mine. This was bringing things home with a vengeance, five thousand dollars being the exact bitter figure Johnston himself had sold the mine out for shortly after discovery!

The longer his thoughts cruised around through these tales the more mixed-up he got. With so much smoke wasn't there bound to be fire? Unlikely as Micaela's contentions appeared, he was no longer certain they held no truth at all. There were more dang fools in this world than you'd figure. As he very well knew, having turned up a few with his own flights of fancy. If there was any substance at all to her claims might not that blue quartz have come from a mine — this same Salvation she insisted had produced it?

But lost for three hundred years?

That took some swallowing. At least the Dutchman had been rediscovered, three times that he'd heard about. How come this one hadn't?

Yet you could understand that if you looked at it soberlike. Actually the mine had never really been lost — not if she had hold of a map . . . just abandoned, you might say. And you could see all right how this might have happened if you could believe the Peraltas were sure enough descended from that Baron Whatzisname.

Spanish kings — particular Philip V — had made quite a habit of handing out land they had never set eyes on to folks who could do something practical for them. There were plenty of land grant cases in the courts, though none he had heard of as gutsy as this, trying to grab a whole territory, you might as well say.

Johnston couldn't believe they would ever get away with it, no matter *who* backed them. It didn't stand to reason. And it was like this fat dude, he thought, to be fully aware of this if he was raking in shekels for cooked-up quitclaims the way the girl claimed. Why, the slippery son could live like a lord if he got enough chumps to pony up in that fashion!

Oberbit's scowl turned morosely reflective as he peered at the ins and outs of this deal, seeing new vistas opening before him. Any feller that figured to have all his marbles should be able to work out some way to get in on the manna in a setup like this. Easy money was whoever's could latch onto it.

He lagged along for a spell until the girl was beside him. "This mine," he mentioned, "this lost Salvation you're figurin' to stake. Is it just a big blow-out or is it spread around kinda, with likely ground strung out at both sides?"

While she was trying to pin down the gist of this McCready, loping up, said in his irritating pulpit tones, "Plenty of room for extensions," and Micaela said, "Oh, yes!" smiling brightly at Oberbit. "On thees we are counting."

Oberbit stiffened, eyed the fat man suspiciously.

But the lawyer, unperturbed, declared confidentially, "Don Manuel's estate has many irons in the fire —"

"Has it now?" Oberbit growled, looking

sneery. "I got the notion from what Micaela said that her ol' man died owin' such a wad there wasn't even a pot —"

"My dear fellow," expostulated the dude, "do have a care how you throw words around. A young lady raised as Miss Peralta has been . . ." He let that drop to say somewhat abruptly, "It was the *entailed* part of the Peralta estate I had reference to. Don Manuel, as far as ready cash is concerned, was indisputably up against it. But this does not mean he was entirely without resources. He had lands, a hacienda, a hundred peons at beck and call —"

"Which, accordin' to her, was sold off to satisfy his —"

"Not quite all." McCready smiled. "There were a lot of intangibles concerned with matters we are not prepared at this moment to go into. You are not to assume Miss Peralta is penniless. Considerably reduced from what she is used to — yes, quite considerably, but hardly to be spoken of in the same breath with you."

His smile broadened smugly. "We are still in control of the Casa Grande Improvement Company, the Salt River Valley Irrigation Company and a number of other remunerative assets, including the Peralta Grant, which we will prove in the courts is a quite substantial part of her inheritance."

Oberbit felt like he had stepped through the Looking Glass and was about to be confronted with Alice's talking rabbits. He rasped a toil-roughened hand across his scraggle of beard stubble, blew out his cheeks and pushed again into the lead.

The sun was down out of sight now, and the desert's swift dusk was beginning to thicken like smoke in the canyons. It behooved him, he reckoned, to put his mind on the business of getting them out of this maze. But he couldn't help thinking that if McCready didn't honestly believe every word he was saying, the feller ought to get the king's prize for actors. While not ready to swallow the lawyer's fantasies in toto he was too much impressed to call them downright lies. Some parts of this anyway looked bound to stand for truth.

Point was, which parts?

He blew his cheeks out again, muttering two or three underbreath swear words, and prodded old Tallow Eye into stepping out faster, with his own gaze irritably hunting for Pine Mountain. Near as he could recollect, from here on in this trough they were traversing ran arrow straight — a few bends maybe with a handful of forks, but easy enough stuck to if a man kept his eyes skinned. About the last thing Oberbit wanted right now was to discover himself lost in these killer mountains.

Midnight passed and a moon came up to mingle its argent shine with the stars' glint to make their surroundings look even less real. Johnston pushed on, stopping only occasionally to rest the tired horses, wanting always to have some edge in reserve. Just in case, he told himself, eschewing elaboration.

One o'clock came and drifted creepily behind them. A swooping bullbat startled Micaela into frightened wakefulness and on some far crag a coyote yammered like a soul in torment.

McCready, presently coming alongside, wanted to know how much farther to Sunflower. "I can tell you better when we git to Pine Mountain," was Oberbit's answer. "You sure as hell ain't fixin' to stop, are you?"

"A good meal and clean sheets could do a lot for that girl."

"They ain't got no hotel, if that's what you're pinin' fer."

"I thought maybe," McCready said, "there might be some mail for me."

"If you had mail sent there you're just

askin' fer trouble. My advice is forgit it."

"You got a thing about that place?"

"I got a pretty agile memory."

"Well?"

"Last time I was there it wasn't what you'd call healthy. A little argument popped up and after the guns cooled they had to bury three fellers. You in a buryin' mood? That burg is headquarters for some pretty tough characters."

Nothing more for the moment was said on that subject. McCready dropped back to jog for a while beside Sammy and his open-topped holster, looking taciturnly thoughtful. The fat man appeared to be doing most of the augering but in so low-voiced a fashion the words ran out of wind before they caught up with Johnston.

Not that he gave a hoot. What he'd said about Sunflower, while not strictly accurate, wasn't far off the truth. Maybe they hadn't actually buried anybody but the blame couldn't be fixed on any lack of trying. Guns had been fired and the racket turned pretty obstreperous. The facts were that Oberbit, strongly concerned with personal survival, hadn't stuck around long enough to learn what the score was. He was satisfied in his own mind he had dropped at least two of them.

McCready, if he stopped, was like to find out how rough rough could get. Strangers in that kind of place were plumb set up to be prime objects of suspicion. The big trouble with owlhoots was they generally played for keeps.

XI

A more fitting label for the windswept huddle of shacks and corrals called Sunflower would — in Oberbit's opinion — have been Horsethief Basin because, without scraping too fine a point on it, about the only plausible reason for anyone's sticking around a roost of that kind was to keep track of stock being rested in transit from someplace on the Blue, where every second rider was some kind of rustler.

Everybody knew those fellers were on the make. In these days, before Burt Mossman was called from New Mexico to come pin the deadwood on the more obnoxious, all Arizona was largely an owlhooters' paradise. The country was flooded with the cut-and-shoot gentry hotly run out of better-run places. Maybe Curly Bill's influence hadn't got this far north, but there were dozens of others cut from the same cloth who would do anything to turn a fast buck. A careless man's life wasn't worth a plugged nickel.

Perhaps something of this had been

brought up by the dude's pistolero in that guarded palaver they'd been having back there. In any event the next time McCready loped forward again it was to declare rather prissily that he would forego his mail and for Johnston to make their next camp on the Verde.

"The Verde *River?*" demanded Oberbit, scowling.

"What's biting you now? Don't tell me your qualms extend in that direction, too."

Oberbit pulled his gray mule to a stop. "Nope. But I'll tell you somethin' else! I'm a-gittin' fed up with the dragfooted way you've been nestin' on the secret of where-at we're bound fer. I ain't stirrin' another single dang step till I'm told fer sure where the hell we're goin'. Now roll that up in one of yer stogies!"

Color rushed into McCready's plump face. His eyes winnowed down and his mouth clamped shut like a door being slammed. But he must have sensed in Johnston's defiance the man wasn't going to be put off any longer.

With a sourish look that stopped just short of contempt he said, "That's where we're going. To the Verde. Let's get on with it."

"And that's where this mine is?"

"That's where the mine is."

"Whereabouts on the Verde?"

"Just find it," McCready said, "and throw up a camp."

Before Oberbit could press the matter further, the girl, coming up, said, "I've had about all I can take for tonight." Then, suddenly stiffening, twisting her head, she peered peculiarly at Johnston. "What's the matter with him?" she asked with her glance sliding back to McCready.

"He wants to know where the mine is."

She brought her stare back to Johnston. "Can't it wait until morning? You'd have to build up a fire to see anything now."

"Well," Johnston said, "then we'll camp right here," adding doggedly: "I didn't hire out to pilot no goose chase! If I'm your pardner then by grab I've got rights!"

She looked kind of vexed, not to mention dog-weary. "Of course you have rights — no one's trying to deny them. But I've got some, too, and right now I'm so . . . Fix my bed, will you?" She gave up a wan smile. "In the morning, I promise, we'll all study the map. Then you'll know as much about it as we do."

Oberbit, though he doubted that last, set about getting the loads off the packstring while the dude, locating her bedroll, moved off a short ways to start putting her tent up.

He didn't look ready for much more of this himself, was probably just as well pleased that Oberbit had stopped. The gunfighter, glancing at Johnston, winked.

Which he found almost as remarkable as Micaela's newly demonstrated linguistic ability.

He called out to McCready, "Which watch you takin'?"

The lawyer, frowning, rasped his jowls and said irritably, "Can't we forget about that just this once?"

"No skin off my butt." Oberbit grunted. "It was you that pushed playin' sentry — not me."

He looked around to find out what the gun artist thought of it but Sammy Darling had taken himself out of sight. He never had laid himself down with the rest of them, always off to one side, like any nearer would contaminate him.

Oberbit, snorting, rolled up in his soogans. Seemed like he hadn't scarcely got his eyes shut when a hellamonious racket of gunfire clawed him out of his covers like a jack-rabbit jumped from a pile of brush. Grabbing his six-shooter he peered around wildly in the dawn's fog-patched light.

Luckily nothing moved or in his half-awake state he'd have thrown down for sure.

The girl's voice cried from the tent, "What is it?" and the lawyer, with his face poking out of his blankets, grumbled, "Seemed like it came from off there someplace," and stuck out a hand in the direction of the horses, none of which were missing.

They were all there for sure and every one of them staring prick-eared through the stringers of fog toward the last ridge they'd crossed getting over here last night.

Johnston, sheathing his pistol in the waistband of his pants, got into his boots and picked up a rifle. Ghostly steps moved nearer behind the fog that was holding the horses' nervous attention and Oberbit hastily slung up his Winchester.

"No need to shoot," declared Sammy Darling, breaking from cover. "Only thing needed now is a shovel."

He grinned at their blank looks. "Lucky I decided to keep myself available. Them Paul Prys that were follerin' finally got up enough steam to make it to the ridge back there. I dusted one but the other sloped like an Irish hunter goin' over the hurdles. Mebbe," he said, tipping the nod at Johnston, "you better come take a look."

That there might be some sort of status symbol, even if left-handed, in the hired gun's calling on Johnston instead of the man who paid his wages did not occur to Oberbit. The possibilities inherent in this unwanted development were too urgently in his mind at the moment to leave much space for any fringe thinking.

In a fine sweat, gripping his rifle, Oberbit strode off into the fog after Darling, cursing under his breath the stupid cupidity which had put that foolhardy pair on their trail. He didn't care whether they'd been shot or not except as it affected the one who'd got clear. *That* was a piece of unfinished business they'd be bound to hear more of as soon as the departed could beef up his hand.

The stringers of fog were beginning to lift as the sun rose over the tops of the cliffs to put its burning-glass rays on the ridge crest. The far side though, where Sammy stood beckoning, still showed long-lying patches of fluff like wool in the zigzagging hollows.

As Oberbit joined him, the lank pistolero loosed a wet splash of amber and, shifting his cud, said with dry wisdom, "Some guys never learn to know their own luck. If he'd stuck to hoss tradin' he could be shovin' his feet under a table about now."

The dead thing on the ground with the red on his shirt-front had just a short while ago been Moses Kelly. The Lexington liveryman had sold his last saddle and wouldn't ever get up from where he was now.

Oberbit, dragging a hand across his chin, allowed, "We better pile some rocks on him — no sense ruinin' a good shovel in this stuff. You git a look at the other one?"

Sammy let go another squirt of juice. "What I wanted to see you about. It was him — this other one — that got off the first shot. Threw down soon's he seen me. I'd of knocked him ass over elbows only, just as I squeezed, this clown crossed in front of him." He poked Kelly's shoulder with the toe of a boot.

"You get enough look to know him again?"

"I'll know him," Sammy said. "About my height, some thicker through the waist . . . not much neck. Texas pants an' a Texas hat. Southpaw — hook-nosed bastard come within an ace of fixin' my wagon. Blue cowboy wipe, knotted to the right, pulled tight beneath his jaw."

He shifted his chew, spat again. "Know him?"

Oberbit seemed to have a little trouble swallowing. "You were lucky — real lucky. That guy ain't no slouch. Name's Weminuche Bill. Used to be boss guard at the Mountain Maid Mine."

XII

Darling looked to be turning that over. "Friend of yours?"

Johnston's eyes rolled around. "I wouldn't figure it that way."

"What you think he'll do now?"

"Probably light out fer Tombstone. One thing fer sure — he'll be back. You can count on it."

The gunfighter scowled. "Might not be a bad idear to keep him under our hats for a spell. Wouldn't want that dude to git no wrong notions —"

"Like mebbe you wasn't quite up to yer job?"

"Like mebbe you better put a smile on your puss if you're goin' to go 'round makin' cracks like that."

The purr in his voice sounded kind of unsettling and the snout of the cannon whipped out of his holster made Oberbit say without beating around any bushes, "I know when to keep my lip buttoned up!"

"If you don't it could get buttoned permanent, bucko." With a significant look and a jerk of the head to cue Johnston for travel, he fell in behind and they struck out for camp.

McCready's stare was crammed with questions. Micaela was up, standing right at his elbow, eyes solemnly round, hands nervously fingering the front of her dress. "Well, speak up!" McCready growled, eyeing Johnston. "Did you know him?"

"Moses Kelly. The guy who sold you the horses."

"Is he . . . dead?" Micaela asked.

"He looked plenty dead to me," Johnston answered, and the lawyer said, "We better get out of here fast."

When no one objected he even pitched in to take down the girl's tent while the unruffled Sammy lent a hand with the packing. In no time at all they were moving up the wash toward the now clearly visible bulk of Pine Mountain.

Weminuche Bill was much on Oberbit's mind, though he kept his thoughts on that subject to himself. One thing he was convinced of: if the man's curiosity had prompted him this far he would certainly be back to pick up their trail and the next time they saw him was nothing a man would want to look forward to.

For two cents, Oberbit told himself bitterly, he would cut his string and shake the dust of this outfit. But he knew, of course, even while he said it, this was just wishful thinking. He was hooked and he knew it by that piece of blue quartz. Wild horses couldn't have dragged him far from Micaela so long as she had a map which might turn up more of it.

When they got out of this gulch and had cut to the left, skirting enough of the towering lump of weathered granite to hide them from any possible skulkers camped on the backtrail, Oberbit pulled his gray mule to a stop and spun up a quirley while waiting for the others to rein in around him.

With a knee crooked around the horn of his saddle he put away his tobacco sack, scratched a match and fired up. "Well," he declared through a full head of smoke, "reckon it's about time we had a look at that map."

"We can't look at it here!" McCready said testily.

"*I* can, an' will," Oberbit spat back, "or you kin dang well try gittin' there by yourself," and he put his adamant look on the girl.

Micaela blushed prettily. "Dan, he's right. I promised —"

"But that Kelly business changes —"

"It ain't changed nothin' fer me," Johnston told him. "Dig it up or we part right here."

The lawyer glowered, swelling up like a toad. "You'd go off and leave a poor defenseless girl alone away out here in this trackless waste? A helpless orphan raised in a —"

"She won't be alone unless you abandon her. All the help you could ask fer ain't much beyond the far side of this mountain if you're chump enough to trust 'em. Give you a chance, too, to pick up that mail you was settin' such store by. Sunflower's off yonder not more'n five miles."

He picked up his reins. The girl said, "After all, it's my map — I don't wonder he's suspicious. I say show it to him, Dan."

When he still didn't move she cried, plainly vexed, "You said your own self we've about reached the place where it will have to be deciphered."

Still McCready hesitated, this very reluctance tending to enhance the map's validity regardless of any value it might turn out to possess. And, if it did nothing else, it obviously whetted Johnston's determination not to budge from his stand until he'd had a good look at it.

Pulling his lip, the lawyer appeared to commune with his thoughts, irritably struck by the prospector's likeness to the hairy face of that waggle-eared mule; finally, tight mouthed, he produced a legal-seeming envelope from which he drew a foxed and much handled fold of paper that looked in some danger of coming apart at the seams.

With considerable caution McCready unfolded it. "Careful," he muttered, handing it over in a manner that suggested more than just ill-concealed reluctance.

The thing was more detailed than Oberbit expected, the course of the Verde plainly marked and spelled out in Spanish. Sunflower appeared at the northeast edge with O'Neil Tank below it and, further due south, another tank without a name. But nowhere could Johnston discover any X.

Diamond Mountain, Black Mesa and Round Valley were labeled. Maverick Mountain and Indian Springs Canyon were easily picked out with Red Mountain below and Granite Mountain to the west perhaps a couple of rough miles. Alder Creek was marked and had a bull's eye flanking it with Black Ridge marked above it. Where the creek emptied into the Verde's horseshoe bend there was a Maltese cross.

Oberbit, looking up with a scowl, said, "This thing don't mean a heap without there was some kind of measurements to go by. Where are the directions?"

The lawyer said in clipped tones, "Where they won't get lost."

"Good. Let's have a look at them."

McCready, thinly smiling, flicked lifted brows at Micaela. The girl said reasonably, "The map is what I haff promise to show you. Have you not seen it? *Bueno*. The instructions are better left where they are. We weel tell you where to go . . . how many steps thees way or that."

"Do you think," shouted Oberbit, "I'm goin' to run off with it!"

"Certainly not." McCready, exchanging hard looks with his pistolman, announced spider-soft, "You will not run anywhere. Without I say so. Does that clear the air for you?"

Oberbit, though not a man to pass up a challenge, was far from the fool a lot of folks took him for.

The issues here were too clean cut for argument. Nobody but a chump was going to fingerwave Sammy after the recent demonstration he'd provided with lead and powder.

Though it went sore against the grain to

back down and left him feeling like a belly-crawling sidewinder, Oberbit climbed off his stump with considerable alacrity when the rusty-faced Sammy slipped a grip around his gun butt.

"Okay, okay," he mumbled through a scowl. "Where do you figure I should take you?"

"Just so we understand each other. The thing to remember is we're all in this together. In toto, as they say in the courts. Though half the mine's yours, when and if we record it, control of this venture will remain in my hands." He smiled with a suggestion of smugness. "Just where on this map are we standing right now?"

Oberbit took a surly look at his surroundings. He would like, by grab, to know how it was that whenever he had dealings with others he always wound up hunting snipe like a greenhorn. Being patronized was a hard thing to take. By a goddamn dude in yellow shoes and derby it was enough to cramp rats. He'd have given considerable to have had the guts to ram that map down McCready's throat!

He took another hard look at the brush-fringed slopes. "That peak just ahead of us is Saddle Mountain."

The lawyer peered at the map. "It's not marked here."

"You're kiddin'," Johnston said, but nobody laughed.

Swallowing uncomfortably he said, filled with disgust, "We don't go that way . . . got to head south. What part of that map d'you want me to aim fer?" He looked over the dude's shoulder, searching out the bull's-eye. "Alder Creek?"

McCready's smile was bland. "That's as good an aim as any."

"Then we'll drop toward Black Mesa. Be shorter, you'd think, if we cut over to Diamond —" he put a finger on the map — "but this whole country's rougher than a cob. We'll have our work cut out any way you take it."

"Have you been through here before?" the girl asked.

Oberbit shook his head. "No nearer than Sunflower an' onct at that place was plenty fer me." He slanched a glance at the lawyer. "How you goin' to git the stuff out if we find it? By mule pack?"

"We'll worry about that when we find it," McCready said. "How far's this Black Mesa?"

"Mebbe three miles if it was flat as a table-top. Way it is, probably nearer to seven."

"And then what?" the lawyer said, revealing his impatience.

"Then we'll head fer Indian Point . . . which would be about here on the map if they had shown it. Should be a trail that will get us to Alder, if I know Injuns."

"We goin' to reach this creek by dark?" Sammy asked.

"More like sometime tomorrow if we play in luck."

McCready looked at him and sniffed. "A man makes his own luck, Johnston. You better see that it's good and, while you're at it, better do something about any tracks we might be leaving. Shooting people isn't the best kind of answer when you're fumbling around trying to locate a mine. A smart man endeavors to remain inconspicuous."

XIII

They camped that night at Indian Point, all of them glad enough to call it a day. The country hereabouts was worse cut up than a slawed head of cabbage, all up and down, boulder strewn, treacherous and bristling with catclaw and cholla that cared no more about drawing blood than the kind of folks that hung out in dark alleys.

It was still light when they came onto this place, but only just. The jumbled horizon wherever one looked was a chaos of darkening crags and peaks, about as wild looking a region as anyone with half his marbles would care to be in. The only proof Johnston had that they were where he said they were was a scattering of blackened circles on the ground which he claimed to be the evidence of old Apache fires.

The girl looked around her nervously and shivered. The lawyer's face was clamped like he had bit into something obnoxious. Only Sammy seemed impervious to the desolation around them. He helped Oberbit unload the pack horses and went off to gather wood for the fire while Johnston set out his pots and pans.

Somewhere a cougar screamed but Oberbit's thoughts were no farther than six feet away, where McCready had just dropped an armload of branches. Incongruous as McCready looked in yellow shoes and derby with that cigar stuck in his face and the crazy cape flapping in every shift of the wind, Johnston found himself mildly astonished to discover how little he was inclined toward laughter.

He had met some queer birds in his peregrinations but none that he couldn't get some kind of line on — until he'd bumped into this outlandish shyster.

The man was a bundle of contradictions. Take that last bright remark if you wanted an example! "A smart man," he'd said, "endeavors to remain inconspicuous." Talk about purple camels! And if he was so goddamn set on keeping himself invisible why had he picked Sammy Darling to travel with?

Might be a fine way to cope with trouble, but the last kind you'd want if you were trying to avoid it. So what did that make McCready? Certainly not any white dove of peace!

Oberbit banged his ladle on the side of the wreck pan. "Come an' git it 'fore I pitch it away!"

He was a long time getting to sleep that night, and it wasn't just the shift from day to nighttime trying. Thinking back over the hours he had put in with McCready did nothing to brush away the jumpy feelings of encroaching disaster that clawed his bowels whenever he looked at or thought about the bastard. Oberbit may never have shone as a speller but he could pick out a snake as far as he could see one and Dan McCready — for his money, anyway — was already lumped with the two-legged variety.

People, you realized, were not always consistent, but there were entirely too many facets to this yellow-shoed dude. All the time *Hurry up! Hurry up!* yet when you came right down to it you could hardly escape the confusing suspicion that McCready, behind his herd of four dollar words, had only contempt for the mine they were hunting. And what kind of sense did that make, for cripes sake?

On the other hand, he'd seemed powerful reluctant to let Oberbit even so much as *look* at that map!

Getting up, Johnston scowlingly rummaged the packs, threw back his head and took a dose of his elixir. And, to be sure of relief, he took another stiffer dosage before slapping the cork in with the heel of his hand.

He got to thinking again then of the girl, this Micaela Peralta, the scion of dons descended from a baron . . . if you were prepared to accept what she claimed gospel. Johnston wasn't entirely sure if he could manage, considering the kind of company she kept, and her variable accent. Yet he recognized that her claims *could* be made in good faith — she wouldn't be the first apple blossom to be plucked and made the innocent dupe of some unscrupulous schemer.

He stood ready to admit that appearances, no matter how bizarre or truthward leading, were not always borne out by the facts. Though he didn't suppose anyone would believe it, he was himself a graduate of the Golden School of Mines. His guise of ignorant desert rat was a kind of protective coloring adopted on the theory: "When in Rome do as the Romans do." He had not stumbled into finding the Silver King — or the Bull Weevil, either — simply on the strength of a smile from Lady Luck.

So maybe this Micaela was a Peralta of the Peraltas — stranger things had happened in the course of his experience. But for a girl who'd spent most of her life in a convent she seemed pretty hep to a number of things not ordinarily included in that kind of curriculum. She might quite naturally have leaned on her old man's lawyer, but she had sure as hell never heard of Oberbit Johnston in faraway Guadalajara!

He was up at first crack of dawn, not exactly bushy-tailed but certainly looking forward to settling once and for all how much of a mine he could level his hopes on. Sammy Darling, hawking and spitting, went off in the brush to attend to his needs before stepping over to wake up McCready. The dude, when he'd pulled himself together, roused the girl and, by the time she returned from a wash with canteen water, Oberbit had the grub forked onto their plates.

The lawyer didn't appear to be in such a tearing rush as he generally was to get away from camp. Maybe he figured Moses Kelly's demise automatically took pursuit off the itinerary. If he did he was liable to be in for a jolt. Nothing was for sure with a pelican like Weminuche Bill, who came from a long line of hard-nosed forebears, all believers — like McCready — that a man made his own luck. Of course the dude didn't yet know about Weminuche, so while the lawyer was indulging himself in an after-breakfast smoke, Johnston set off for a piece of high ground just to make sure doubly certain. For the moment.

It seemed the same notion had occurred to the pistolero. Oberbit found him hunkered by a rock combing the landscape with a cavalry glass. "Which way's that jigger apt to come up from?"

Johnston shook his head. "I'd sooner predict which way a frog'll jump. He'll be back an' with help, that's all I'd be be sure of." He stood quiet a bit, peering. "What's the chances, you reckon, of turnin' up that mine?"

Darling grunted, still searching the slopes.

"You been around them longer'n I have," Johnston grumbled. "Looks like you oughta have some idea anyway."

The gunfighter grimaced. "What's your estimate?"

"Funny setup. Still, I can't see there'd be much point to 'em lyin'." Johnston pawed at his face where the whisker stubble was beginning to itch. "If there ain't no mine why the hell git us out here? Feller don't outfit a trip just fer laughs."

"You heard him." Darling spat. "He's got irons in the fire he mebbe ain't flashed yet."

"Like what?"

"If I knew that," Sammy said, "I might could raise a strike. Let's get back."

McCready, apparently, had finished his stogie. He was striding up and down, the picture of impatience. In a put-upon voice he demanded to be told why he should be wakened in the middle of the night if they weren't planning to leave this broiler short of sundown.

"We're leavin' straightaway," Darling told him. "We was just checkin' up the traffic hereabouts."

The lawyer's eyes sharpened. Oberbit, observant, said, "No sign of anyone nosin' our trail. Which don't have to mean much."

Sammy Darling spoke up. "You're in good hands. No need to worry. You got two sets of eyes watchin' out for your interests. With the best hired gun in the West it's a breeze."

The dude gave the lanky man a long cool inspection while Johnston went off to round up the horses. "What you think of that fellow?"

114

"What's to think?" Sammy countered. "Just another Joe Blow. He'll do what you tell him. Long's I can breathe on him."

The girl in the meantime had gone after Oberbit. While he threw on the packs she watched sort of wistful. "I wish I could do some of these things," she said finally.

Oberbit, looking surprised, declared, "Nothin' to it — just a matter of practice."

"Could you teach me?" she asked as he handed over her reins.

His stare flashed admiringly. "I'll make a point of it, ma'am, soon's we git this here mine producin'."

She got into her saddle, still watching him oddly. "Supposing it's played out?"

"You got any reason fer thinkin' it might be?" Oberbit spoke a bit sharper than he'd aimed. And the girl looked confused, but only said, "I sometimes wonder."

She turned away then, leading McCready's horse over to him. Sammy Darling came up to put the show on the road. Oberbit said, calling out to the lawyer, "You still minded to fetch up at Alder?"

McCready nodded. "Where the creek empties into the Verde, if you can get us through this labyrinth of bake-oven gorges."

"I just hope," Oberbit said, "there'll be a mine when we get there."

★ ★ ★

It proved a heap more work than anyone had thought for, and more time consuming. Around four o'clock Johnston told McCready, "We ain't goin' to make it tonight; that's for certain. You want to knock off? Way it's been going I doubt we'll see the Verde this side of tomorrow noon."

While the lawyer was glumly digesting this Sammy Darling said, "We might as well lay over," and Micaela sighed her agreement. Nobody suggested posting a guard but after he'd got the supper things taken care of Oberbit found himself a high spot, where he was joined by the rusty-faced Sammy. But though they kept a sharp watch until the light grew too poor, they failed to uncover any sign of other horsemen.

"You can't bank on that," Oberbit grumbled. "Someone could show five minutes after we're off this hump. There could be a dozen of 'em lyin' in them breaks right now. I'll watch till ten. You can take it till two an' wake McCready to take the last turn. I'll give in it's a nuisance an' like enough a complete waste of effort. I don't really look for trouble till we've turned up that mine . . . if there is one."

Darling didn't register much enthusiasm

116

but got up when Oberbit nudged him. "Hear anything?" the lanky gunfighter asked.

"Lot of crickets — wolf or two. I don't expect there's been time fer him to git back yet. But like the feller said, when Injuns is closest is when you don't hear 'em. Weminuche's that kind. Wouldn't be surprised if some of his maw's folks did most of their walkin' around in Apache boots. Better keep yer eyes peeled."

He was never rightly sure which of the two of them failed to keep his eyes open. McCready woke him just as the first wimpy gray began to dilute some of the solider dark. Oberbit used some of last night's wood to get the fire built up and broke out his skillet. They put away the grub without needless talk, none of them at their best this early. While Darling scowlingly redded up the camp Oberbit went off to fetch up the horses.

Most of them had learned to come when he whistled. This morning, however, not a one ambled up — only old Tallow Eye, his ratty gray mule. He found them soon enough though, each with its throat cut.

XIV

He called McCready and the others, let them look for themselves, and saw Micaela's cheeks blanch.

"But who could haff done thees thing?"

Johnston's glance, passing around, peered hardest at Darling. "You reckon," Darling said, "it could've been Weminuche?"

"I think he'd skin his own gran'ma if he thought she'd bring a profit."

"But to keel our *caballos* . . ." The girl wrung her hands.

McCready, eyes swiveling suspiciously from one to the other, demanded irritably to be told what they were gassing about. "Feller Sammy saw two-three days ago — or thought he did," Oberbit muttered. "Wasn't noways sure but the description tallies. Kind of a caretaker at the Mountain Maid —"

"And what would he be doing out here?"

"Keepin' cases on us, it looks like. Could've been with Kelly fer all we know. I wouldn't bet there ain't more of 'em if word's got around we're onto somethin'."

The lawyer said, frowning darkly,

"Wouldn't Kelly have been more likely to strike off alone?"

"Never was the kind to play a lone hand. He's a dealer," Oberbit answered as though this covered every loose end in sight. But Darling growled, "Who's to say what kinda guff Johnston dropped while he was traipsin' around buyin' up that camp gear? Whole town is probably buzzin' with it now. If them two had teamed up I'd of seen them together." And he slugged Oberbit a look that left the blame around his neck like the Mariner's albatross.

Oberbit shrugged. "Can't make an omelet without breakin' eggs. I got roped into this right in front of that peckerneck."

"If you hadn't shown him that paper —"

"Crying over spilled milk won't put it back in the bucket," Micaela pointed out. "The thing we've got to decide now ees how we're to get there without any horses."

"Shank's mare," Oberbit grunted, adding when she looked puzzled, "reckon we'll just have to use the legs God give us."

This did not set any better with McCready than it did with her. Dismay was bright in her stare. The lawyer with his face turned florid said, "She can ride your mule."

"Not today. Grub'll be ridin' the mule,

along with the skillet, the pots an' the beddin'. If she wants to hang onto a stirrup, that's okay."

While the lawyer, affronted, was skinning back his lips, the girl said, pushing her chin out, "That's all right. I don't expect to be pampered just because I'm a woman," but the look she gave Johnston would have withered an oak post.

Darling, enjoying this, grinned at the both of them. Oberbit, turning kind of pink around the gills, could have shrugged it off if that had been the end of it. But seeing the way he looked, Sammy couldn't resist adding, "Thinkin' it over, I ain't sure he didn't kill them broncs himself."

That was too much for Oberbit. He took after Sammy like hell wouldn't have him.

With one quick swipe Darling fisted his pistol. Equally swift, Johnston flung himself aside and came up with a swing to the chin that lifted the gunfighter clear off the ground. His head jerked back and the rest of him went after it, the gun departing his lax hand as, tangled in his spurs, the man went heavily down.

Johnston kicked the gun skittering into some prickly pear.

"Now git up and try sayin' that again if you feel lucky!"

120

"That's enough," McCready squeaked with the cloak flapping around him and his eyes bulging like a pair of squeezed grapes. A short-barreled derringer gripped in a chubby fist waved Johnston back peremptorily. "If you miserable brush poppers can't get along —"

"I've already quit," Johnston said, glaring back, but the girl wouldn't have it.

"You *can't* leave us now!" she cried, eyes enormous.

"The hell I can't."

Darling picked himself up with his ruptured pride, as venomous looking as a trampled snake. With his lips peeled back like a savaged horse he spoke in unforgiving tones: "Never put your hands on me again."

"Hoo hoo!" Johnston jeered, and stalked back to the camp where he dug his bottle from one of the packs and near half emptied it in his riled condition before the girl, catching up, managed to talk him out of leaving. The clincher came when she pleaded, gripping his arm as though she'd never let go, "Who can I trust if you run out on me — *you*, my own partner!"

Peering into the green eyes of that desperate face, Oberbit gulped and was lost. For what she said was truth; you couldn't get around that. If he took off she'd be at their mercy. It made him understand why she'd given him half the mine — she had to have someone to stand up for her. Left to themselves that pair would steal her blind! — if they hadn't already.

In this new concept he could not help wondering again about those horses. It *did* seem a little mite early for Weminuche to have got all the way to Tombstone and back. McCready could have slaughtered those horses himself — it was at least as reasonable as some of the other things Oberbit couldn't find the why for. Who knew what a forked stick like him would do?

"All right, I'll hang an' rattle fer a spell," he growled, inexplicably embarrassed. She took her hand off his arm and he moved back the better to get hold of his breath. Young things always had managed to find his softer spots, and she was pretty much of a looker in her odd and foreign way.

"Here's your mule," McCready said, tossing him his reins. "Just hand back that paper before you take off out of here. We've got no use for absentee owners."

"He's changed his mind," the girl said, chin up again, and McCready said dryly, "Now I wonder what prompted that?"

He peered a moment at Johnston, looking through and beyond him as a man sometimes will when his mind's on something else. "It doesn't appear to make a great deal of sense to kill our horses yet leave our stores and water untouched." Sniffing irritably he said, "I don't like it."

"Whyn't you write your friend Barton about it?"

Ignoring this pleasantry the lawyer said, "If they wanted to put us out of business . . ."

"Could've been a warnin'."

"You mean a hint we're not wanted?"

"Some of these back-country critters ain't what you'd call real partial to strangers. Might be their idea of flaggin' the trail — a hint of worse things in store if we don't take off."

McCready studied him. "Think that's it?"

"No."

"I don't either," McCready barked. "If this Weminuche feller is a pal of yours —"

"Pals like him I kin git along without." Johnston pawed at his face. "Best explanation fer killin' them broncs is to slow us down; that way we'll be easier to keep a eye on. I doubt whoever's behind it's tryin' to stop us; I'd say they got it figured we're here fer a profit. Any stakin' that's done they want to be in on."

The lawyer chewed at his lip. "Question is, can we stop them?"

"I thought that's what you fetched Sammy along fer."

The dude's glance thinned but all he said was, "I'll have him give you a hand with that truck." Swinging around on a heel, cloak fluttering behind him, he went waddling off and, someway now, he didn't seem so preposterous.

Ten minutes later they shook the dust of that camp, Oberbit in the lead with old Tallow Eye breaking trail, Micaela next with McCready close by, and his paid pistolero bringing up the rear, each with a canteen over his shoulder, each with a hand gripped fast to a rifle. As Oberbit had said, in this kind of country a man never knew. With the loss of their horses still fresh in mind they aimed to be ready should there be more surprises.

A man could be on his guard against harassment but thwarting an assassin was something else again, and Oberbit's confidence in discussing the horse slaughter did little to bolster his own flagging spirits. He was filled with a disquiet he couldn't rightly account for, a feeling of unease that seemed to grow by the hour.

He had never been one to try to fool himself. He believed the apprehensions that had hold of him went deeper, were more complex, than any enmity aroused through the set-to with Sammy. That the gunfighter would bitterly nurse trampled pride was a foregone conclusion, but there was something at work here more hackle-raising than that . . . something tied in with that mine and McCready.

He didn't trust the lawyer any farther than he could heave him. There was more to this thing than the crackly yellow map the fat man had shown him — how was it the girl had entrusted *him* with the instructions instead of carrying them herself? Could it be, Johnston wondered, that she hadn't any choice? That the whole urgent business of this safari was McCready's?

He could see how that might be. The lawyer, going through her old man's papers while settling up the estate, could have come onto the map and accompanying instructions. He wasn't the kind to overlook a main chance no matter what else he might happen to be.

The more Oberbit rolled this around the more likely it seemed that the whole driving force behind this wild venture must have stemmed from McCready's discovery of the map. He could have drawn the girl out, fired her imagination, convinced her that only by reclaiming this forgotten mine could there be any means of security in her future. He could urge that without its promise of wealth he would have no means of prosecuting her claims to this Arizona land. She was young, inexperienced, entirely at his mercy. . . .

Yes, that must have been the way of it. A private talk with Micaela seemed suddenly urgent if only to settle the doubts in his mind.

He looked around, still thinking, but more carefully now. The lay of the terrain seemed conducive to mineralization. Most of the biggest producers these days had been located in regions quite similar to this, so rugged as to be almost inaccessible. It would cost quite a pile to put adequate roads through, not to mention the machinery for opening the mine — always providing, of course, it was worth such an outlay.

The day warmed up as the hours dragged by. This was grueling work. Almost half the time that was getting away from them had to be spent in recuperating strength, though the girl was holding up remarkably well.

They nooned on Alder Creek where it splashed and gurgled around the side of a mountain, Oberbit watching every one of them for tricks.

He had about cleared the girl in his own mind, but his uneasiness extended even to her. The phony accent — all that pidgin lingo that she seemed to put on, and take off when she forgot herself — continued to make him not entirely sure of her.

Even a girl brought up in a convent might occasionally have to struggle with a language wholly foreign to her, but it hardly made sense that in the grip of strong emotions she always got things straight.

XV

As it happened, his chance for an off-the-record palaver came sooner than he'd looked for. He was squatted, scouring his pots at the edge of the stream, when she sauntered up in aimless seeming fashion to drop her piece of blue quartz *kerplunk* between his spread-apart knees. "I'm theenk perhaps you had better take care of thees."

In the midst of his suspicions he felt a little embarrassed by such obvious trust. His jerked-up glance found her staring at the water, watching the ripples with the fascination of a child. Swift changes of light reflecting off the stream seemed to lend her face an elfin quality, a sort of little girl look astonishingly at variance with the full-breasted earthy ripeness of so willowy a grown-up figure.

Her eyes in this light appeared as green as emeralds. Even rumpled and tired as she undoubtedly was from so many hours of bucking the brush, there was a freshness about her, a kind of unspoiled something that dug deep into him.

He reached down for the rock, picked it up, flushing, frowningly shoved it out of sight in a pocket. He was rusty with girls, befuddled by her nearness and the richness of what he thought to have glimpsed in so unguarded a moment. Her hands came up in an expressive way to touch her hair and sweep it back from her face. Her lips relaxed and she seemed to be smiling at something caught in the drift of her thoughts; and she was like a vessel filled to brimming with all the things a man could ever want.

Her shoulders, straightening, swung more toward him though her eyes continued to mirror the creek. She said with her lips barely moving, "You must trust me, Johnston. It ees not like you theenk."

"An' how would you know what I'm thinkin'?" he growled.

"You could not help but theenk there ees something peculiar in a girl who hunts for her mine weeth a lawyer and a man who makes his living by shooting peoples."

Well, she had something there. Peculiar wasn't half what he thought! "First off, then," he said, "you can drop the poor little rich girl act an' put your cards face up on the table. Just tell me, straight out, what the hell's goin' on."

Her cheeks had paled but her eyes, coming around, looked as frankly direct, as personal as his own. "I am afraid of him, Johnston. Afraid of what he'll do if —"

All the breath hung up in her stiffened shape, she brushed past him, hurrying off wooden-faced in a spin of swirling skirts.

"Well, Johnston," McCready said, spider soft, coming up on his other side as Oberbit stared after her, "I thought you'd be getting around to it before long."

"Huh?" Oberbit, staring blankly, found things coming too fast.

"It will do you no good to go honey-talking her. Any prospects she's got — until she's of age — will have to pass through my hands," and he smiled thinly, smugly. "By her dear father's will I'm executor of his estate. You'll find she can't move a finger without my consent."

Oberbit looked baffled. Then his eyes scrinched to cracks as the dude's thought unfolded. His hands balled into fists. "I oughta knock them goddamn teeth down your throat!" He said in a fury, "What'd you take me for?" and advanced belligerently.

The fat man backed off. "Now wait a minute —" He swallowed nervously with his hands out in front of him. "I've dealt with fortune hunters be—"

Johnston said, outraged, "One more crack outa you like that . . ."

McCready threw up his hands. "All right — all right! I made a mistake —"

"Be goddamn sure you don't make it again!" Oberbit snarled and, still fuming, strode off to repack the mule.

It was midafternoon when they got onto a bench that disclosed their first view of the confluence, the place where the creek emptied into the Verde River. It had occurred to Johnston after he'd got away from the fellow that the one sure way to have removed McCready's suspicions would have been to give up that half interest she'd given him — not that he was about to be such a chump!

Anyway, the lawyer had approved that, hadn't he? McCready's own hand had passed him the paper. Likely he'd figured this a kind of insurance, an unbeatable means of binding Oberbit to them — of making certain he didn't run out in a pinch. But as he saw it now there was no guarantee he'd be allowed to depart with his half of whatever.

Johnston's thoughts were rudely jolted back to the present when he saw the complex of corrals and buildings beside the lake where the two streams met. His glance found McCready's face a study all too easily deciphered. Oberbit, scowling, said, "Is that where we're supposed to hunt fer this windfall?"

McCready didn't answer but got out his map. They were standing in brush some two miles from what appeared to be a ranch headquarters and no small operation. There wasn't much likelihood of their presence being discovered without they went nearer or just plain got careless. Oberbit, peering across McCready's shoulder, found no lake on the map and began looking around for some other handle to orient the picture.

Where the two streams met, a bosk on the map was marked *cottonwoods,* but in the scene before them only one tree showed. A huge old bugger, it must have been five feet across at the bole where it stood above the lake's far edge just in front of the shabby clutter of buildings.

He eyed the landscape again, his quartering glance singling out a rock spire thrusting out of the lake some twenty-odd yards from its nearest end. And there on the map this was labeled *stone butte.*

Johnston nudged the lawyer. "We ain't looking fer that mine near them buildin's, I hope."

McCready turned a flushed face. "You'll know all about that when I'm minded to tell you. Stay here with the girl," he snapped and, beckoning Sammy with a jerk of the chin, struck off sourly grunting up the side of a slope.

Johnston watched them rim out in a thicket of shaggy juniper, where they crouched, heads together, either discussing the unwanted buildings or, more probably, the advent of interlopers where they'd looked to find untrammeled desolation. Crusoe discovering the footprint could not have been more perturbed than that derby-hatted son of a bitch.

The angry grumble of McCready's carrying voice found echo in Johnston's own disquiet. Any search for lost mines is hardly a project that commends itself to a sharing with neighbors, and if the thing they had come for was in this vicinity any blind fool could foresee complications.

The pair came down, McCready's fat face looking ugly and baleful. A fine sweat was on him, the roll of his eyes like a stallion bronc's. "We're going over there," he said in his prissiest voice and snatched up a rifle, but Oberbit caught hold of him.

"Mebbe you better peek around some first. By the looks of that place it's no piddlin' outfit. Might be bitin' off more'n we can chew."

"What I been tryin' to tell him," Sammy growled.

McCready, glaring, grudgingly took a halfway tuck in his temper. He sarcastically said, "You got a better notion?"

"If I was runnin' this I'd let 'em come to me."

The lawyer pushed that around, fidgeting and scowling, and while he was doing it Oberbit said, "As a full half partner in this here mine it kinda seems like it's time I had a look at those instructions. I think it's time we all discovered just where-at this mine's supposed to be. Happens it's close and we're goin' to have to work in full view of that outfit —"

"Close!" McCready's harsh laugh rang out like a bark. "If I haven't misread the directions completely the goddamn mine is under that lake!"

XVI

Sammy, plainly enjoying this, said, "There's a pretty pass."

Micaela and Oberbit exchanged startled glances; consternation had dropped both their jaws.

Reaching inside his suitcoat — the map passed to Johnston with the girl at his elbow — McCready produced the small yellowed sheet with the quill-penned instructions. "Twenty steps south from a bosk of cottonwoods," the lawyer read, squinting and scowling, "between the lightning-struck pine and strata-streaked stone butte; turn right down arroyo forty-seven paces to brown knobby rock the size of a sea chest. Turn left at rock and bearing on brushy mountain due west — Are you following me?"

"I can follow the map," Johnston, grunting, muttered, "but most of this stuff seems to be under water."

"Then it seems we agree." McCready looked at the girl.

"I can see a brushy mountain," she said,

peering and pointing. "I can see a streaked butte sticking up from the lake and one lone cottonwood at its far end. I don't see any arroyo . . ."

"Me, either." Sammy grinned.

McCready took umbrage. "What do you find that's so funny, Darling?"

The gunfighter smoothed out his rusty-cheeked face. "Well, nothin', I guess. Kinda struck me there I might wind up the only dang fool to make a nickel outa this."

McCready took a long look at him and, finally sniffing, went back to fingering his dog-eared list. "The arroyo, obviously, is under that lake. The rest of the directions fetch us up against what was probably its east wall. 'Under a rock overhang half hidden by bushes is the mouth of the tunnel opening,'" he read, and put away his paper.

"So we don't even know," Johnston said in disgust, "if there *is* any mine. Or — if there ever was one — that it isn't worked out." He kicked at a horse apple, fetching up a bitter glance. "What did you want to go over there fer?" he said with his look jumping across to the buildings.

"Regardless of whether there is a mine or isn't," the lawyer said, "that ranch was built on patented ground that is all part and parcel of the Peralta Grant."

136

"So you thought," Johnston said with a curling lip, "you might find a buyer fer one of your quitclaims."

The lawyer glared. "Not quite," he said looking down his nose. "As executor of the Peralta Estate I thought it high time they found out where they stood."

Johnston's thoughts, leaping ahead, took a second hard look. "They've got an equity there —"

"They're trespassers, man! They haven't a pot to spit in!"

"One thing they have got, you kin bet, is *guns*, an' they might not be a bit reluctant to use 'em. I think I'd be a little careful was I you."

"Two can play at that game," McCready growled, eyeing Sammy.

"He's just one man, no matter how good he is. If he gits within reach he could damn quick git buried," Oberbit said, not much caring if he did.

Sammy Darling spat to show his contempt.

The lawyer, grimacing, said, "We'll see what develops. We'll go over there now before his crew gets home. We got a couple hours yet," he added, glancing at the sun. "Shouldn't take long to find where we stand."

Oberbit grunted. "You don't need me. I'll stay here with Micaela."

"We're *all* going," McCready rapped. "A show of strength never came amiss. For all they know we may have a crew, too. A firm hand —"

"We won't look too damn firm walkin' into that place."

McCready plainly had the bit in his teeth. Oberbit decided to quit wasting his breath. "All right," he growled, "lead on MacDuff," and picked up his rifle.

They went in skirting the east side of the lake. Johnston kept his eyes peeled, but the ranch seemed deserted till they got into the yard. As they started across it a gimpy-legged ranny stepped out of the cook shack, mouth open, to stare. "Anybody home?" McCready hailed.

"Where the h— Excuse me, miss," the man mumbled, discovering Micaela. "What I mean is *where*'d you come from?"

"Came from our camp, of course," the lawyer told him. "Who's running this outfit?"

"Jubal Clee."

"Where's he at?"

"Big house yonder," the cook said, pointing.

McCready, wasting no further time with civilities, struck out for the gallery, the other three following. "Hello, the house!" he called as they came up, and put a set of knuckles against the open door.

"Come in — come in," a voice gruffly bade. "Straight down the hall."

Oberbit, thinking this reception kind of odd, dropped a hand to the butt of his six-shooter as he followed the others down a door-lined corridor that gave into a combination sitting room and office. The walls of this sanctum were decorated with stuffed animal heads, the pine board floor with Navajo rugs. But it was the man he looked at with a small sense of shock, surprised to find him ensconced in a wheelchair.

Big he was from the waist on up, powerful shoulders on a barrel torso with a neck like a bull and a pugnacious jaw and steel-trap mouth below bitter eyes that looked about as friendly as an unsheathed knife. A blanket covered him from the belt on down and he had one hand out of sight beneath it. He plainly wasn't one to beat around any bushes, because as they all crowded in he said, "What do you want?" about as gruff and unflinching as the whole hostile look of him.

"You Jubal Clee?"

"That's my name."

McCready showed a parched smile. He

139

wasn't about to waste time going around a barn, either. Crisp as you please, he announced, "This young lady is Micaela Mariquita Peralta y Moro. In case you don't know it, this spread you've built up is on her property. We're here to discover what you intend doing about it."

The man's heavy shape had stiffened belligerently, eyes squeezed down to glittering cracks. A cigar was gripped between his teeth and he rolled it across them, peering through the dribble of smoke with as baleful a look as might have come from a cougar whose young have been threatened.

A pine knot on the fireplace hearth exploded, the light swelling and rippling across the low ceiling, against whitewashed walls. Over the mantel a cavalry carbine and heavy-hilted saber hung half crossed above the faded lithograph of a man in full uniform — old General Jeb — under whom perhaps this man had once ridden; he looked old and indomitable enough.

He showed more restraint than Oberbit had looked for. "What gives you the notion I'm on her land?"

"I'm not talking of notions, I'm discussing facts. She's the last of the Peraltas in male line direct to Don Miguel Nemicio, first Baron of Arizona by decree of Philip the Fifth when that Spanish king by royal edict gave him the title and the lands to support it, the same legally recognized January 3, 1758. Fact number two, we have the documents to substantiate this. Fact number three, since your ranch is well within the borders of the original grant you've no right to be here save the right of use — a squatter's right," McCready said contemptuously and thrust out a finger. "I advise you to vacate no later than tomorrow."

The man looked as though he were about to strangle. His face darkened up like a rotting berry, his eyes looked about to roll off his cheekbones — it would not have surprised Johnston had he leaped from his chair. But the man got hold of himself to ask, furiously, "And if I don't?"

McCready said suavely, "We're not here to make threats. We're simply stating our position. If you want to remove yourself amicably we'll pay fifteen hundred dollars for your improvements —"

"Get out of my house!" Clee cried with blazing eyes. "Get off my ranch!" The very temperature of that room seemed to drop beneath the stare of those outraged eyes. The blanketed hand appeared behind the bore of a pistol. "Put foot again on Roman Five and there won't be enough of you left to bury!"

XVII

Back where they'd left Johnston's mule and what supplies they had not been forced to jettison, the girl, moodily silent since leaving Clee's headquarters, abruptly spoke her mind.

"All this way, and what have we to show for it? Three hundred years! We never should have come; the thing was hopeless from the outset."

Her censuring glance, loaded with resentment, rolled off the lawyer like his cape was thatched with feathers. "Oh," he said, "I wouldn't call it a fiasco yet. One can't help, of course, feeling a little depressed, finding the mine under water and that ranch on top of it, but this jaunt hasn't been entirely without emolument. The" — he grinned at Oberbit — "Silver King's contribution alone has more than taken care of all expenses to date, and the benefits from other quitclaims — not to mention our arrangement with the Pacific Improvement Company — have sweetened our account by at least a hundred thousand."

"Of which I have not seen one cent!"

McCready looked as pained as though he'd been accused of stealing it.

"My dear," he said, "of course you haven't. As executor of your father's estate I am charged by the Court with taking care of it for you — you know all this, we've been over it before. You are clothed and fed, your every need anticipated."

"I would like to see some tangible —"

He threw up a hand. "I am accountable to the Court. Any speculations undertaken in your behalf are narrowly scrutinized. Searching out the many facets and documents needed for a successful prosecution of your claims to this land is not without considerable expense, even diligent as I have been in not incurring them. But in the interest of all concerned, let me assure you that when you come of age every penny shall be accounted for," he said with a great deal of dignity.

The girl, grimacing, turned away without reply; and McCready said, "If I may say so, Johnston, I think we'd all be the better for some food under our belts."

"You aim to eat *here?*"

"Certainly we'll eat here."

Johnston, scowling, took the man aside. "You ain't figurin' to go on with this, are you?"

"We didn't come out here to turn around and go back just because some fool waves a gun in my face."

Johnston peered at him, astonished. "In my time I've run up against a few of these cow bosses. You can look down your nose an' curl your lip if you want, but that guy wasn't just shoutin' to hear his head rattle!"

"Fine." McCready grinned. "A real all-wool, genuine first-run bastard is just what the doctor ordered." Chuckling, he gave Oberbit a poke in the ribs. "Quit holding your breath. We're not whipped yet."

"You get a look at that bunkhouse? He's got at least a dozen men in his crew and if they're not tough hands I'm a Chinaman's uncle."

The lawyer settled his stare on Oberbit with the kind of look most men wouldn't stand for without it came from their wives.

"I'm beginning to think your reputation has been grossly exaggerated," he said.

Oberbit flushed.

McCready finished: "If you want to pick up and get out of this don't let me stand in your way."

They heard Clee's crew ride in about dark.

Johnston feverishly wondered if the

144

lawyer really knew what risk they ran, squatting here in plain sight of that outfit's headquarters. He had sat up with his rifle long after the others rolled into their blankets, convinced there'd be trouble before the night was out.

But there wasn't. Nothing happened. No one, apparently, even scouted their position. It wasn't, he thought, like Clee to ignore them. He'd told them to get off his ranch and they'd defied him by spending the night here. Not many cowmen would tolerate that.

He hadn't looked like the kind to make empty threats, so what was holding him? McCready's palaver about the Peralta Grant? That didn't seem likely, yet it began to look as though the lawyer had some reason for his confidence until, along about midmorning, three men climbed into saddles in the Roman Five yard and pointed their horses toward McCready's camp.

Sammy, spotting them first, threw a wink at Johnston before alerting the lawyer. Oberbit, ignoring the gunfighter, put the mule on a pin and took up a stance beside the hand-clenched girl. "Stay away from the rifles," McCready said, cautioning Darling. "It's their move. Let them make it. I'll do the talking."

Sammy showed his twisted grin, though he left a fist dangling beside the butt of his pistol. Oberbit's poker face told them nothing. The girl looked like she wanted to run.

"Nice morning," McCready said as the three reined up.

There was no mistaking the delegation's leader. He sat his horse in the middle as though he had been glued to it, a big-jawed man with beefy shoulders and a temper that showed in the cut of his mouth. He settled his stare on the lawyer. "Thought you were told to get off this ranch."

"Was I?" McCready smiled.

A gray shine of satisfaction brightened the surface of the man's slate eyes. "You're bein' told now. Pack your gear and start movin'."

"Sounds like you haven't been told the position," McCready said smoothly. "I'm Dan McCready, executor of the Peralta Estate. You must have heard of the Peraltas; your outfit's squatting on Peralta land."

"Is that a fact?" The hard eyes swept across watching faces. "This," the man said, slapping his thigh, "is a six-shooter. Handiest thing we've found for settlin' claims. If you're not out of here inside of three minutes it's going to start talking."

McCready's mouth tightened. "We can get a court order."

"You just do that, mister," the range boss said, taking out his watch. "Meanwhile — if you value your health — you better get movin' while you've still got the chance."

Oberbit didn't think this ranny was kidding and McCready, apparently, got the same message, for with a riled show of teeth he pitched in his hand.

"You tell Jubal Clee that when we come back it will be to stay. Pack up!" he growled in a black snarl at Johnston.

The Roman Five boss nodded. "Two feet under and two across will be all the land you'll get around here."

"You should of let me plug him," Sammy Darling said when the Roman Five trio were no longer in view.

"The odds weren't right," the lawyer said grimly, "but we'll take care of that," and the twist of his face showed he was putting his mind to it.

They must have walked three-four miles before he said, suddenly smiling, "There're more ways than one to get the skin off a cat. Pull up — we'll stop here," he growled, and Oberbit groaned.

"We don't even know if there is a mine."

"We'll take care of that, too," McCready said gruffly. "You still got that blasting powder?"

Oberbit stared. "I fetched along a can, but if you're meanin' what I think you are —"

"We came here to find and open up a mine. We can't work a mine that's buried under water. We've got to drain the water off."

"But Jesus Christ," cried Oberbit, gulping, "you think that bunch is goin' to stand fer that!"

"We'll find out," said McCready, smiling. "One can ought to do it."

XVIII

At the earliest chance to do it unnoticed, Johnston dug out his spare bottle of rat killer and stoked his courage with almost enough to ward off the chills. He wasn't really one to put much store in Dutch courage, you'll understand; with him it was more in the nature of a habit, like swatting at flies or standing up to pee.

He'd sworn off several times, regular as clockwork, and just as persistently he'd begun another habit. Whenever he felt the urge coming on he'd stash away a quart or a pint, depending on what he could afford at the moment. He'd got pretty adept at hiding the stuff, conscientiously sticking to whatever pledge he'd made, stoutly refusing to touch a drop until he had achieved the promised time limit. After which, with just as much thoroughgoing application, he would proceed to empty where it would do the most good each and every saved-up bottle, these toots sometimes lasting a whole hand-running fortnight.

But when boon companions had finally deserted him and the town's soberer citizens had crossed him off their charity lists, along with the fickle goddess of luck, Oberbit, cursing, had given up trying. What the hell was the use? You could just as well hang for a sheep as a goat! Death, he'd seen, was the common lot, and a man might just as well grab at it happy.

Not in his wildest dreams, however, had Oberbit figured to wind up in this fashion. What McCready proposed was tantamount to suicide without even the possibility of changing your mind.

He thought a long time about dumping that powder or making out maybe it had someway got lost, but several daunsy looks at Micaela's blue quartz wouldn't let him destroy his last hope for that mine. He would sooner have cut off his right hand, he guessed, than go away from here without even knowing.

Just before dark McCready called for the powder. "You brought plenty of fuse and whatever, I hope?"

"We got enough to do the job. You sure you want to try this?"

"You know any other way to take off that water?"

"You could offer to cut them in," Oberbit

said lamely. The fat man looked his contempt without speaking.

Johnston took a deep breath. "Whatever else happens you can damn well bet that bunch won't set around twiddlin' their fingers. They'll come down on us like hell with the clapper off!"

"Just keep your mind on draining that lake," the fat dude advised. "What happens afterward is my responsibility. You don't have to stick around. Just blow that dam and you can pile on your mule and make far apart tracks."

Johnston, scowling, was more than half minded to say where he could go. Instead he growled, "There's a bit more to this than blowin' holes in a dam. Drainin' that lake ain't going to empty no tunnels."

"So we'll get pumps," McCready said just as though he'd forgotten the Roman Five completely. "You got any other pointers you think I'd better hear?"

Oberbit, swearing, went off to fetch the powder. Sammy tramped after him. "What the hell do *you* want?"

"I got my orders," Darling told him. "I'm stayin' right with you till you git the job done."

It occurred to Johnston to wonder yet again if there was one grain of truth in this whole frigging thing. But as before, if the mine were a hoax, he couldn't see where McCready stood to profit.

The girl, coming up, took hold of Oberbit's arm as they were about to set off. She thrust a rifle into his hand. "Be careful," she whispered and going onto her toes reached up and kissed him.

He was so knocked in a heap that she was disappearing into the shadows before he got back enough breath to swallow. But she had left him with plenty to chew on anyway.

By the time they got to the lake and to the place he had picked, the night was as dark as a black cat's overcoat. The lights of Roman Five glimmered like jewels from the half lit buildings across the water. Johnston thought to himself that it was too damned quiet, but there wasn't a blessed thing he could do except make the best of it and hope like hell they could keep themselves hidden until he got the fuse sizzling.

It was scary enough trying to clear out one hole without tripling the risks with multiple charges. The dam was primitive, just earth and rock, but it had been here long enough to become just as solid as the lake bed itself. Properly blown, one hole should do the trick. The big problem, of course, was how to get it far enough in without making noise enough to bring that bunch down on them. It was straightaway apparent that Sammy had no intention of dirtying his hands.

"Only reason I'm here is just to make sure you don't run out short of gittin' the job done."

"Great!" Johnston said and, forthwith ignoring him, got down to business.

It was touchy, patience-fraying work trying to get anywhere while having to be careful to remain undetected. He would sooner have tried with a hacksaw blade to saw himself out of an iron-barred cell — at least trying that wouldn't get a man killed. He had to clear a bigger hole than the can's actual measurements; he kept running into rocks that had to be lifted out. First off he'd tried burrowing under one only to come slap-dab up against another. It took him two hours to set the can deep enough to offer any likelihood of accomplishing his purpose. By that time he was wringing wet and about as wound up as a feller could get.

"Pass me in that can," he said, buried to the knees, and Sammy — for a wonder — did his bidding without comment. "Now that fuse," he said in muffled whisper, and a few moments later came wriggling out.

"Ready?"

"Just about," Oberbit grunted, backing off a bit as he paid out the coil. He scooped his hat full of earth and crawled back into the hole, a long ways from certain the rusty-faced pistolero wouldn't even the score with a lighted match. With the loose end of that fuse left out there so invitingly, Johnston wasted no time with last-minute fussiness. He did what needed doing and got out of the hole in a hurry.

Sammy, chuckling in the dark, ran a match across his jeans, poked it at the fuse-end, waited half a second to make sure it was burning and took to his heels.

A hundred yards away Oberbit pulled up and they flung themselves down, panting. In the light spilled out of an open door Johnston saw the Roman Five range boss staring across the lake. They were too far away to hear what was said but a shifting of shadows took commotion to the day pen, where beyond any doubt there were horses being saddled.

Darling said, sounding ugly, "If that thing don't go off —"

It did, with a roar that was pretty near deafening. A white blast of flame lit the

154

surface of the lake. The sound of falling rocks was lost in the rush of surging water. "We better get movin'," Johnston said, and jumped up.

Sammy was all in favor of making straight for their camp but Oberbit, more cautious, talked him out of that. "Tomorrow that bunch'll be lookin' for tracks an' I sure wouldn't want to have them matched up with me. We'd best head in some other direction and take enough time to rub out our sign."

"What good will that do? They won't be in no doubt about who's behind this!"

"Sure. But thinkin' is one thing. Provin' is somethin' else."

"They'll come down on us anyway."

Oberbit, shivering, guessed he damned well was right.

Any guy who didn't need his head looked at would dig for the tules and not wait for nothing. Was a maybe mine worth such Christly odds? And what about Micaela if he decided to run?

He guessed he'd stop long enough at least to pick up his bottle.

XIX

They had heard the blast back at camp and were anxiously waiting when Johnston and Sammy came in looking beat about a half hour short of daylight. "Well, how did it go?" the lawyer, peering, demanded, and Darling grunted, then said, "We didn't hang around, but I reckon by this time she's pretty well emptied. Sound of that water was just like a mill race."

McCready's face showed satisfaction. Johnston said sourly, "I see you've moved the camp to high ground. You reckon that'll keep them Roman Fives off you?"

The fat man grinned.

Oberbit said soberly, "They'll be around pretty soon — I guess you know that."

"You worry too much," McCready said coolly, and fished a cigar stump out of his coat. Rolling it around above the flame of a match, puffing vigorously, he said through the smoke, "You better have yourself a drink and get out of those duds."

Examining his length in the strengthening light Johnston saw what he meant.

All that wriggling around in and out of the hole had put earth stains pretty well all over him — a man wouldn't have to think twice to guess where he'd been. Handing him a blanket, Micaela, looking anxious, said, "Soon as you get out of those I'll take them to the creek."

Too used up to argue, he went off in the brush and came back in the blanket and his long-handled johns to hand the things to her, the stuff from his pockets tucked up under his hat. The girl went off with them and Johnston sat down with his back against a rock, glumly cradling his rifle across blanket-draped knees.

McCready and his paid help moved to stand out of earshot with their heads together, arguing. Oberbit wondered what that pair had up their sleeves, but mostly his bitter thoughts circled the bunch at Roman Five. It stood to reason they'd strike back. An outfit as big as Jubal Clee's had not got that way by turning the other cheek.

McCready had to know this. The man's bold confidence hardly looked the sort to have been built on either shortsightedness or ignorance — you might almost think he *wanted* that bunch to jump him! And that made even less sense than the rest.

He blew out his cheeks and got up to find solace, and went suddenly rooted as a rumor of hoof sound twisted his head. "Stay there!" McCready rapped, and hurried across to join him, Darling fading into the brush.

"Where's he off to?" Johnston growled.

The fat man, turned toward the oncoming horse sound, did not answer, and Oberbit said, "You ever wondered what the end of this'll be?"

McCready looked at him then. "I wonder about many things but never about that." The cold eyes gave Johnston a patronizing look. "If I didn't know where I was going I'd be as windily broke as the rest of you yahoos. And just about as stupid."

Oberbit's cheeks turned dark with resentment but before he could work up a suitable reply the Roman Five foreman rode into clearing and yanked his mount to a stop. The out-of-breath horse was lathered and heaving and the face of its rider showed the rage working in him. "Where's the rest of your outfit?" he barked at McCready.

The lawyer lifted plump shoulders in a shrug. "I never take a roll call before ten o'clock. Something on your mind?"

The man's slaty eyes looked wickedly at him. "By God, I ought to hang the lot of you!"

"Perhaps you'd better come to the point."

If the Roman Five boss was not apoplectic it wasn't for lack of any turmoil inside him. The muscles stood out along his jaws like ropes. His skin turned livid with the fury that rode him and he bitterly said in a half strangled voice, "You'll pay for this, fat man — don't think you won't!"

The lawyer said coolly, "Just what are you driving at?"

"You know goddamn well! You came over there last night and blew our dam. There's not enough water in that lake this mornin' to float a dead mule!"

"Seems to me," McCready said, "you're putting the cart before the horse. Unless you're prepared to prove those remarks . . ."

"Don't give me that! No one else around here would —"

"I'd be careful, if I were you, about airing accusations you're in no position to prove. There are laws dealing with slander and even out here I expect they can be invoked if a man felt sufficiently put upon to hail your employer into a court. The damages —"

With an inarticulate gasp of outrage the Roman Five man whipped the gun from his holster. What he intended was any man's guess. It was never accomplished. Before the gun cleared his hip the flat crack of a shot blew a hole through the stillness. The man on the horse jerked back in his saddle. His arms flailed out, his eyes bulged with shock and with a kind of convulsion he stiffened, lost balance and toppled to the ground.

"You fool!" McCready yelled as Sammy stepped from the brush with a smoking pistol. "I told you plainly not —"

"But the goddamn bullypuss was all set to plug you!" Darling cried, staring like he couldn't understand being hauled on the carpet for an act which, to him, had plainly saved the lawyer's life.

McCready, shaking his head at the futility of explanation, looked resignedly at Oberbit and strode scowlingly across to go down on a knee beside the sprawled shape.

He turned the man over and disgustedly said, "Too dead to skin!" and stood up blank of face to stare down at him a moment as though marshaling his thoughts. "Well, it's done. We'll have to face it," he said grimly, eyeing Johnston.

Micaela came running up with Johnston's

clothes just then to stop, staring speechless at the sight of that crumpled shape with the reins of his shaking horse still tangled in one hand.

McCready said to the girl, "He yanked out his gun and Sammy killed him."

Oberbit licked dry lips and cleared his throat. Micaela looked about ready to bolt. "What do we do now?" Oberbit asked.

"Report it, of course," the lawyer said bleakly. "What else is there to do?"

Johnston could think of several safer notions but ere he could voice them Sammy snapped out of his trance with a curse. "Look," he said thinly, but McCready's black glance left him peering, mouth open.

"We're standing behind you," McCready told Darling curtly. "The man was the victim of a misunderstanding. If anyone's to blame for this regrettable incident it was Clee's man himself, losing his head that way, drawing a gun in so savage a manner. That's the way it was; that's the way we tell it."

It was the gunfighter's turn to lick dry lips. "Couldn't we just put him on his horse an' git outa here?"

McCready gave him a look of cold scorn. "You can't hide a thing like this. Sooner or later the truth's bound to come out, and then where'd we be? Behind bars, charged with murder!"

Sammy looked to be having some trouble with his swallower. Oberbit said, "Who you figurin' to report this to?"

"The man's boss, naturally. We'll take him over there —"

"Jesus Christ!" said Oberbit, staring. "You tryin' to get the whole bunch of us killed? You go in there with him draped over a saddle it'll be open season 'fore you can get the first word out!"

McCready looked at him straightly. "You ever done this before?"

"I don't have to put my neck in a noose to know what'll happen if someone yanks on the rope!"

"Nevertheless," the lawyer said, "we'll do this my way. We would have to go over there tomorrow, regardless, if we're going to lay claim to that mine for Micaela.

"We'll camp there tonight." He held up a hand to stall off interruptions. "Sure, there'll be some hard looks, some irresponsible language, but with their bully boy gone there won't none of them be anxious to kick over the traces." Grin wrinkles showed about the edges of his mouth. "More trouble right now will be the last thing they'll want."

XX

One thing you had to hand him: if confidence were dollars he'd be a millionaire.

How could he be so confounded assured? Was he the par-blind fool he so frequently seemed, just plain lucky, or the slickest bamboozler since Yellow Hair Custer?

Pulled two ways, Johnston called himself seven kinds of loco to be larruping along with such a featherheaded plan. But if the fat man was right Oberbit would be a chump to miss out on his half of the proceeds. Besides, someone had to look after Micaela, didn't they?

Just before starting for the Roman Five, Johnston, gray mule in tow, sauntered nearer to where the lawyer had the girl buttonholed. McCready's back was toward him. Miss Peralta did not look to be enjoying this discourse but was facing him stubbornly, her expression rebellious. It wasn't none of Oberbit's put-in but, feeling the way he did about the pair of them, he drifted casually into earshot.

"Don't count on it," the lawyer was

163

saying gruffly, and thrust out a hand. "You can pass that piece of blue quartz over now."

The girl's angry eyes defied him. "I don't have it."

McCready appeared to be studying her. "I'm not here to play games," he announced, coldly quiet.

Micaela's lip curled. "Do not threaten me, hombre."

The silence stretched thin while the lawyer stood motionless. His words when he spoke struck out like a knife. "So you gave it to that clown!"

She said with satisfaction, "Whoever I gave it to will know how to keep it!"

"Uh . . . what are we waitin' on?" Oberbit said.

McCready came around as though jerked by a string. His wicked stare rummaged Johnston as if half minded to tear him limb from limb. Blowing out his cheeks he yelled for Sammy. "Let's go!"

Under an overcast sky filled with leaden clouds they moved down the last spur in their advance on Roman Five; McCready was in the lead in his ridiculous cloak and derby with the girl, head high, walking by his side. Oberbit, leading the mule, came next. Behind them, towing the victim's pony with its burden of dead freight, Sammy Darling's gangling shape stalked along like a slinking cat.

The nip of fall was in the wind that curled down off the high Mazatzals. That they'd already been seen was amply evident in the disposition of the waiting crew deployed strategically about the yard. All eyes took in the blanketed shape, but if the fat dude noticed he gave no heed.

Oberbit, squinting, slanched a look toward the gallery and was not disappointed. In a rugged and upright homemade sort of chair Jubal Clee sat with a rug around his legs and a Winchester carbine across his lap.

McCready, cool as you please, led past the hard looks of the gun-fingering hands straight up to the he-catawampus himself, the others, though not without divers shades of misgiving, strung out with their trepidations behind him.

"Your foreman wound up at our camp in the brush. He snatched out his pistol shouting a bunch of damned nonsense, but it seems he wasn't quite up to his intentions so we've fetched him back in case you'd like to continue this hassle."

Clee's eyes were awash with the tide of

his fury but he did not make his range boss's mistake. Despite the placement of his predisposed crew something he read in McCready's cool stare kept him rigidly motionless, whatever notions he had tightly held under wraps.

His men watched, reckless looks hunting signs; but Oberbit tried to find in McCready what was holding Clee silent. There was nothing menacing in the dude's easy stance; it was the perfection of studied carelessness. Nor had his tone been remarkable for the promise of dire catastrophes. It must have been the frosty glint in his eyes, that frigid complacence that completely enveloped him as he stood there clearly waiting on Clee.

The cowman's face was ashen, his whole shape rigid with the terrible pressures brought on by indecision.

McCready, it seemed, had called the turn; Jubal Clee didn't look as big to them now. He had paused to listen and it had been his undoing. McCready's bold approach had fed the man doubts, forced him to reappraise the situation and now his advantage had wizzled away. His crew, bewildered — a couple openly disgusted — were no longer ready to stake their lives on the drop of a hat or the whim of a man who'd not fight for his range boss. Clee, hanging fire, had permitted them to think, and they were now disquieted as he was.

Oberbit glanced at the muddy hole left beyond the yard's edge by the vanished lake, his look coming back as McCready said, "We've got work to do here — I'll make a deal with you. Keep out of our way and we'll leave you alone with whatever range lies north of this yard. I'll give you a quitclaim. What do you say?"

No thanks were expected with Clee looking that way, the dull red in his cheeks showing clearly enough what a kick in the guts he found this to be. His stare reached past toward his men and withdrew, looking beaten, and he sat with slumped shoulders, peering into his hands.

"Otherwise," McCready said smoothly, "we'll go ahead and take steps to have this property vacated." He considered Clee. "What's it to be?"

Still the man didn't answer for seven or eight heartbeats. Oberbit was looking for someplace to jump when the cowman said in a throaty rasp, "Let's see your quitclaim," and clamped his mouth shut.

After arranging with the man to buy some tinned stuff and staples to tide them over till they could bring in supplies, McCready told his group, "We'll set up our base at the south shore of this gulch," waving an airy hand toward the lake bed, through the gelatinous mud of which the Verde River still wove its gurgulous, much shrunken way. "Somebody's going to have to ride over to Sunflower and arrange for some timbers and other odds and ends we'll probably —"

"You don't know yet," Oberbit said, striding after him, "if we've got a mine even."

"Better send for a pump, too, while you're over there —"

"*Me!*" Johnston said. "Why do *I* have to go? What's the matter with sendin' the shadow?"

"You're the only one of us who knows the town, or could find his way and has transportation. And you better get started . . ."

"Before we even take a look?"

"Right away," McCready said, peeling off several bills from a sizeable roll, thrusting them into his reluctant hand. "If that mine has been there three hundred years it's a pretty safe bet it will be there when you get back. Take another day of sun at least to firm up that mess to where we can walk on it. If you start straightaway you ought to be back by tomorrow night."

Oberbit grumpily unloaded the mule.

"Better pick up another tent for Micaela," McCready said, "and have them send out a couple loads of siding and three-four hundred feet of two-by-fours."

"Anything else?" Johnston asked sarcastically.

"We could use a couple of carpenters, two kegs of nails and a crosscut saw. And a surveyor if you can locate one." He took another pair of fifties off his roll. "Get a horse for Micaela and another for Sammy."

The girl came over to him just as he was about to step into the saddle. "You'll be careful, won't you?" she asked, peering up at him.

"It's you who'd better be keeping your eyes peeled," Johnston gruffed with a hard look over his shoulder at McCready. "I wouldn't trust that shyster with a dog's buried bone, let alone anything I had any use for." Then he looked at her oddly. "You got any notion who named this mine?"

Her eyes grew round. "Dan McCready."

It figured, Johnston told himself. It gave him plenty to think about plowing through brush that as often as not came clean to his armpits. Everything about this deal revolved around McCready. It was pitiful the way that dude was working Micaela. Her old man must have been milked blind if he had trusted —

A tag-end of motion hauled the chin off his chest and fetched Oberbit straight up in his stirrups. In the tangled patterns of light and shadow he couldn't be sure he had seen a damned thing, but far out on the right at the fringe of his vision he had *thought* to glimpse the fleeting shape of a horse.

And the horse in his mind was Molly McCarthy — Jack McCann's mare that when last seen had been carrying Weminuche Bill!

XXI

He'd had just about time enough to catch them up, but what he would do now that he'd found them was a lot more uncertain than Oberbit cared for. There were several possibilities and none that inspired him to stand up and cheer.

Weminuche was a great hand for grudges and plenty unparticular when it came to evening scores. Yet if he had been sufficiently persistent to come this far any hate he was nursing probably wasn't at the moment as far up on his list as finding out what had fetched them into this region.

He pushed this threat back aways to be thought over later. Right now the chief question in Oberbit's mind had to do with the things McCready wanted from town. The horses for Sammy and Micaela weren't too unexpected and could be used straightaway for packing in supplies; even the nails and crosscut saw made a kind of sense, considering the probable condition of the mine . . . if, he added with a snort, there was any mine and if they were lucky enough to find it!

Lost mines, by and large, were rarely re-discovered. He'd tried looking himself in past years with no more success than the legion of others who prowled forgotten canyons in the dream of fabulous riches.

But, getting back to McCready, two loads of siding and three or four hundred feet of two-by-fours, not to mention two carpenters, argued a degree of permanence that certainly had Oberbit scratching his head. Looking back at the lawyer's casual treatment of the subject, these extensive preparations opened up a number of vistas Johnston hadn't even considered looking into.

According to all he'd heard, this mine, away back, had been extensively worked by Micaela's forebears, more than likely with captive Indian labor. Spanish methods in that far-off time had been pretty primitive, but if this had been the basis of the Peralta wealth he had figured they'd be able to clean out the residue in too short a while to require any buildings.

And what in Tophet did they want with a surveyor!

What kind of dido was that fat dude up to?

Johnston and his mule made a lot better

time on this trip going out than they'd made coming in; not having to lallygag along with a bunch of pooped walkers, they raised the conglomeration of unplastered adobes that was Sunflower about an hour short of sundown, and found it no different than the last time they'd been here — a condition Oberbit nervously hoped would not extend to the populace.

It having been several years since that ruckus he had mentioned, there seemed at least a fair chance he might remain unremembered or that the rannies he'd had trouble with had sought out greener pastures.

He tied Tallow Eye before the general store and keeping his fingers crossed went in. The same potpourri of smells assailed him as he pushed his way through the unchanged clutter. The proprietor lounging behind his counter continued to listen to some tale he was being regaled with by a gnarled old codger tipped back next to the cracker barrel. Johnston, with what fidgety patience he could summon, stood uncomfortably listening, prepared to wait them out if, as generally happened, one tale didn't fold straight into another.

Business perhaps wasn't quite up to par because the broken-nosed gent in the sleeveguards cut in after laughing to ask Oberbit if he was in any hurry.

Johnston allowed he had a long ride ahead of him and would just as lief get started. "I want two full loads of siding an' four hundred feet of two-by-fours driven out to Roman Five soon as may be, an' you can send two carpenters with 'em. We'll also want about two kegs of ten-penny nails. I'll write you up an order for tinned goods an' staples which you can send along with them, and the sooner the better."

Both men were eyeing him in open-mouthed astonishment. The open-collared proprietor pulled at his nose and, seeing as how Roman Five's cook had been in for a bunch of stuff two days ago, asked, "What you feedin' out there, an army?"

"I'm not workin' for Clee," Johnston pointed out. "He's just traded off the part of his outfit that's south of his house."

The storekeeper stared. "I guess you mean the part south of his lake — he wouldn't trade that off for love nor money."

"He ain't got any lake — dam went out." Johnston pushed across his list of groceries. "Tote up what's owin' and I'll settle right now."

They were full of questions, but he left them spluttering and rode his mule to the

Lone Star Livery and picked out a couple of ponies as per orders.

After settling for these, plus blankets, saddles and bridles, which the hostler put on, Oberbit led his entourage back to the store, which he once again entered. The storekeeper's crony had apparently departed, hotfooting it off to spread the news. "I want a tent, an' I'll be takin' it with me — small one'll do, smallest you've got. And you better send out about twelve eight-by-tens, eighteen foot long. The tent and the timbers you can charge to McCready. How soon you gettin' that lumber started?"

"I've got a man working on it. Uh . . . this McCready — you sure he's got an account with us?"

"Executor for the Peralta Estate. You've heard of the Peraltas, haven't you?"

The man's eyes widened, grew blankly narrow as though he were scanning things not in this room. Oberbit said in a cool tone of voice, "This town of yours is like enough squattin' right now on a piece of the Peralta Grant. Might pay you to remember that."

"Yes, sir," the man said. "Er . . . was there anything else?"

"Don't know where I can find a surveyor, do you?"

The fellow's face got boarded up like he had left for the winter. Apparently he didn't even trust his voice but he had enough strength left to shake his head. He found Johnston a folded-up tent and threw in some rope; Oberbit, lugging this, went back to his mule.

He spent several moments pondering, scowling, while his eyes raked the road between this scattering of buildings, peering longest, it seemed, at the Red Tiger Bar. Though there was no one in sight he felt as if half a hundred eyes were keeping cases on him, and though his thirst really rankled he rode past that oasis and turned in again at the Lone Star Livery.

The hostler stepped out with a defensive belligerence. "Somethin' wrong with them hides?"

Johnston slid a look over his shoulder, fetched it back. "Not that I've discovered. No, the horses are all right. Just crossed my mind you might know where I could git hold of a surveyor."

"What you want a surveyor for?"

"Good question. I'll suggest the Peraltas take me into their confidence before sendin' me off on any more errands. Guess I'll just have to tell the boss of this outfit there ain't none available."

176

"I didn't say that. Here, hold on," the liveryman said as Johnston picked up his reins. "Matter of fact, I can run a few lines if it's worth my trouble."

Johnston peered at him dubiously, then said with a shrug, "They're payin' cash money. If you want the work come out to Roman Five an' ask fer Dan McCready. Whatever you'll need you better fetch along with you."

Not caring to risk further flirting with trouble, he struck out for the ranch by cutting across lots, and just when he figured he could draw a free breath there was trouble waiting right in the trail. He was on a black mare whose name was Molly McCarthy.

XXII

"Not goin' to snub an old friend, are you?" called Weminuche Bill with his mouth twisted sideways in a mean kind of grin.

Oberbit stared in open-mouthed consternation. There was no place to run, hardly enough chance even to get started without a man was looking to play target for a bullet.

The ex-boss of the Mountain Maid highgraders waggled his pistol and said, "Looks like we're due for a little heart-to-heart palaver. Just like ol' times, ain't it? Me an' you riding the same stretch of trail." And he threw back his head in a malicious guffaw.

Good living had put a roll of fat about his middle but there was no sign of this in those beady jeering eyes. "What's the matter, Johnston? Cat got your tongue?"

Oberbit tried to sound tough but it came out pretty puny. "Long time no see."

"We're goin' to remedy that," Weminuche said with real satisfaction.

"What do you want?"

"For a starter you can tell me about this strike."

"Ain't been no strike. We ain't even —"

"Next lie from you is going to cost you some blood, chum. A finger for every lie you get caught in." Weminuche, watching him, stepped down from saddle. "Turn out them pockets."

This didn't bother Johnston till he got to the pocket that held the lump of blue quartz which he'd forgotten he had on him until he felt the lump. His chagrin showed at once. Weminuche's gun barrel prodded his gut. "That one, too! . . . Aha!" he sneered, snatching the piece of ore from Oberbit's fist. "Haven't made no strike, eh? What d'you call this!"

"That's a family heirloom the Peralta girl give me —"

"I oughta ram them teeth right down your throat!" Weminuche said, indescribably ugly.

"But it's the truth!" Johnston cried. "Look at the damn thing! You ever see ore in place smooth as that? Took a lot of handlin' to put that much polish —"

"Yeah." Turning it this way and that, holding it up to the light, the man from Tombstone said, "So tell me about it and don't skip a word."

Perspiring, scowling, Johnston told him.

It went sore against the grain to spill his guts in this fashion but with the snout of that six-shooter just beyond reach what choice did he have? This cotton-mouthed Bill would no more care about putting a hole through him than he would about picking his nose in public. "We ain't found the mine yet," Oberbit said in conclusion.

"You will," Weminuche urged with unction. "You will if you know what's good for you, and I'm not goin' to be fobbed off with half of your half. When you get around to recordin' your claims the first extension — the one nearest the vein — you'll stake out for me and put my name on it."

He twisted his mouth in an evil grin. "I'll be watchin' you, chum. With a glass and a rifle. Be sure you don't let an old friend down."

Oberbit was halfway back to the ranch when he remembered the pump he was supposed to have ordered, but he had things considerably more serious prodding the flurry of his pinwheeling thoughts. The hateful face of Weminuche Bill with its saturnine grin seemed to peer out at him from wherever he looked.

Where were the other tough hands he'd

gone back for when Sammy had cut down Moses Kelly?

The one paralyzing question uppermost in his mind and which gnawed every minute without being asked was what Weminuche would do if Johnston crossed him up. He didn't have to ask that. It was all too apparent. The man might not succeed but he would sure as hell try!

Bedeviled by this conviction and the probability that the fellow's companions were keeping sharp eyes on McCready right now, he pushed on to get back, not stopping for anything. If nothing untoward had happened he could sleep when he got there, reassured by the hope they might still pull this off.

He was shaky with relief when, just before sunup, he crested the last rise to find the camp still intact, having feared Jubal Clee, spurred by frustrations and trampled pride, had got up from his paralysis to avenge lost face and reverse McCready's coup.

But the cold gray light of early morn disclosed no sign of such visitation; there was no activity across the hole of that emptied lake, except a curl of smoke from the cookshack stovepipe, to indicate the man's crew was even up.

As Oberbit rode into camp with his horses on tow, Darling stepped from a clump of squatting cedar, his rifle in hand. "You stayed all night in that town fast," he said, coming up. "I don't see no lumber — you must've come back with a chunk of fire."

"Lumber an' grub'll be along later." Johnston paused to say darkly, "Weminuche's back. Probably watchin' us now through a glass someplace."

If he was concerned by the news Darling failed to show it. Without looking around he said, "How many with him?"

"I only saw him."

"No sweat," Sammy said on the edge of a grin. "If he was as tough as you think he'd of stayed in the first place. He knows which side of the bread gets the butter."

Oberbit hobbled his horses and staked out the mule where they'd have no trouble seeing him, shouldered the tent and walked toward the ashes of last night's fire. The girl was awake and got up when she saw him. "How did it go?"

Oberbit shrugged. "I got most of the stuff. Want me to put this tent up for you?"

"That Johnston?" McCready called. Micaela said it was and the fat man, throwing off his blankets, came across in his shirtsleeves, looking around with a scowl. "I thought —"

"Save your breath. Grub an' lumber's coming out later. I fetched the horses an' tent an' found you a feller that says he can run lines. Only thing I didn't take care of's the pump — no sense orderin' that till we know what we'll need."

The lawyer eyed him a moment without comment, finally putting out a hand. "I'll take care of that tent."

Oberbit gave it to him, wheeled off and built up the fire and, while it was readying, opened tins of corned beef and stirred up some batter, suddenly hungry enough to eat a dog with the hide on.

They got through breakfast without altercation, Darling eating with the rifle across his knees. If they were watched from the ranch it was not apparent, though it seemed rather likely Clee's curiosity to find out what they were up to must be keeping someone busy.

"How'd you find Sunflower? See anyone you knew?" McCready asked when they were finished.

Oberbit answered, "I ran into Weminuche."

The lawyer said, "Is that a fact? Put the finger on you, did he?"

"He gave me a look at the snout of his pistol."

The fat man nodded. "Then he probably knows as much as you do. What kind of deal did he try to screw out of you?"

"Said he wasn't settling for no half of my cut. Wants the first extension."

Surprisingly, McCready grinned.

Oberbit, shaken, finally said in a growl, "You wouldn't, by God, be fixin' to oblige him!"

"Why not?" McCready laughed. "Be one way to get the fellow out of a grudge fight."

"You're sure plenty free with things that don't belong to you," Oberbit said in a scowl of resentment.

The lawyer said coolly, "That paper you've got calls for half the Salvation. It doesn't say anything about extensions. Whether he gets it I think should depend —"

Micaela, cutting in, said, "I side with Johnston." And Oberbit, considerably encouraged, declared, "Payin' him off is no way to rid yourself of a blackmailer. That feller's twisty as a basket of snakes — he's one of the reasons they had to close down the Mountain Maid! Highgraders were drivin' 'em batty so they hired Weminuche to pick up some tough hands and put a stop to it. He stopped the fellers that was stealin' 'em blind, then him and his bunch took up where they'd quit!"

"Why didn't they fire him?"

"I guess they were afraid to. You'll damn well find out if you bring him into this."

McCready, still smiling, shifted his shoulders in a shrug. The girl said, "When are we going to start looking? Before we start bickering about who gets what it seems to me only sensible to find out what we have."

McCready, looking dubious, considered the arroyo. "Still looks pretty sticky. Another day —"

"You wait another day," Oberbit told him, "and that highgradin' whippoorwill may move right in. When he hears about what happened to that lake it won't take him long to decide where the mine is." Peering out across that mudcracked bottom with eyes suddenly narrowing, he cried, " 'Pears to me like somebody's *already* been lookin'!"

XXIII

Following the point of his shaking hand, they all saw what had upset and outraged him, the dug-in track of somebody's boots coming over the lip of the yardside shore and descending catty-cornered over the dun expanse of that gummy bottom to climb out the west side in a series of treacherous slips and falls that left a plain story for all who would look.

McCready was frowning. The girl looked shocked. Sammy Darling, who'd come up to see what had grabbed their attention, shifted his cud and his voice thick with disgust said, "One of them Roman Five peckernecks probably. Must've gone through some time in the night — else I'd have seen him."

Johnston, jerking out of his trance, broke away to go hurrying around the south rim, heading for where the boots had climbed out. He reckoned Sammy was right but a man had to know. If those tracks had been made by someone not in Clee's outfit they had likely been left by some pal of

Weminuche's, and there was no chance like right now to find out.

Splashing across the Verde's course he waded through water almost up to his navel before he got out on the stream's far bank. If he was right in his remembrance of what he'd seen on the map the side concealing the mine tunnel ought to be directly across the arroyo.

He plowed to a stop and, shading his eyes, took a long appraising look. He did not see anything resembling a tunnel or even the mouth of a half filled-up cave, but the wall dropped sharply from what looked like an overhang. And down on what had so recently been the bed of the lake, some sixty yards this way from that wall, was a knobby looking mound. The rock that was supposed to look like a sea chest?

With a lifting excitement he looked over his shoulder and eyed the brushy mountain. He had a hard time restraining himself from going down straight off but prickly thoughts of Weminuche finally dissuaded him. He guessed he could wait. They were not too well fixed if it should come to standing off a clutch of claim jumpers.

He moved on to the place where the tracks climbed out and stood a while staring from scrinched-up eyes. He needed to think, to sort things out, but too many notions kept after each other in a dizzying whirl until they all ran together to increase his confusion. He built a cigarette and lit it and pitched it aside with a frustrated growl.

There was no lack of sign. Two or three guys had stood here waiting and when the tracks' maker joined them they had all gone off toward a thicket of mesquite beyond which the ground appeared considerably cut up by horses. The tracks went south along the Verde's east bank.

Oberbit was so filled up with notions he couldn't think which way a man had ought to jump. Following those tracks seemed the quickest and most practical plan for whittling that hardcase down to size, but the question of who had cut across that arroyo looked of equal concern in shaping future policy.

The mark of those boots plowing through that mud suggested some tie-up between Weminuche and Roman Five. There might not be. There might be no more to this than an attempt on the part of Weminuche's bunch to scout out the lay of things, find what they were up against. But these muddied boots had come from

Roman Five, which could mean that someone from Clee's outfit had crossed to make contact, or set up some deal, with this Tombstone bunch.

Yet even this appeared open to doubt. Contact could and most probably had stemmed from Weminuche. The horse sign here and those waiting men seemed to argue that one of Bill's understrappers had approached Roman Five by some other route, done whatever he'd gone over there for and run into something which, for speed or concealment, had forced him across that muddy arroyo.

Sammy Darling came up and took a hard look around.

"What's it look like to you?" Johnston asked.

"Trouble," Sammy said, and Oberbit nodded. "Do we go after them," he grumbled, "or go see what we can get outa Clee?"

Darling scowled. "How old would you say them tracks are?"

Johnston squatted down and ran fingers through the dirt, picked up one of the horse buns and consideringly broke it. "Three, four hours." He jerked his chin toward the Roman Five yard, where a couple of hands had stepped out of the cookshack

189

and turned to watch them.

"Come on," Sammy said, and struck off heading north around the rim of the arroyo. When they came to where the tracks left the Roman Five yard he passed the rifle to Oberbit and, tugging his hat down, let hard eyes follow the prints till they were lost among others about a rope's length from the main house's gallery. He started moving that way.

The pair of hands drifted up. "You lookin' for something?"

"Go tell Clee he's got company."

The pair exchanged glances. With a shrug one departed.

The other one said with a belligerent scowl, "Things is some different than the last time you come by."

"You bet," Sammy said, bleached eyes looking him over through the cracks of scrinched lids. "This time one of you could damn well git hurt."

Jubal Clee came onto the gallery, wheeled in his chair by the hand who'd gone after him. He got a stogie from his pocket, stuck it into his face, put a match to its end, held the match in his hand, narrowly inspecting its dying flame. He looked up to say bitterly, "What is it this time?"

"We struck a bargain with you," Sammy

Darling said quietly. "It has been my experience some pretty unpleasant things generally overtake welchers."

The cowman's neck turned dark below the bulge of his jowls. Temper rushed into the boil of his stare and it cost him an effort to hang onto the confidence with which he'd intended to deal with this hired pistolero. He pulled a long breath deep into his lungs. "I don't know what you're talking about."

"Then I'll make it real plain," the gunfighter told him. "Last night someone leavin' this yard crossed the bed of that lake, climbed the west rim and went off like old buddies with whoever was waitin' there." He held up a hand. "Before you try to weasel outa that maybe you better send someone to have a look at them tracks."

Clee spoke like a man who had been hatefully affronted. "You trying to tell mc now who I can talk with and who I can't?"

"Old man, who you talk with couldn't bother me less. Nor what you do. But any deal hatched up between your outfit and that bunch in the brush that came down here from Tombstone will be taken by the Peraltas as complete cancellation of any and all understandings between us."

The cowman's livid stare slanched an

191

irascible look beyond him; and McCready said, coming up beside his shadow, "That's about the size of it, Clee. If the weight of your spread is thrown in any way against me you'll be dealt with as trespassers and treated accordingly."

The cattleman cried in a shaking voice, "If you think you can come in here and threaten —"

"No threat's been intended. You may regard it as a promise," the fat man said, grimly wheeling away, a jerk of his jaw pulling Oberbit and the gunslammer after him. Then he stopped to turn a bleak look across his shoulder.

"We're reopening a mine on this property that's been in Miss Peralta's family for three hundred years. You're being served notice that we intend to work it, that our activities in this connection will likely bring in a flood of footloose fools who may not prove conducive to either peace or good will. We'll do what we can to see your rights are respected . . . so long as you diligently live up to your agreement.

"One further piece of advice: prowlers will be shot on sight."

XXIV

The search for the lost Salvation, when McCready finally got around to it, took considerably less time than one might have imagined. The arroyo lake bed was hardly a quarter mile across by maybe twice that length north to south. The points mentioned in the map were not too difficult to locate, with both the butte and Brushy Mountain rearing up in plain sight. Oberbit found the tunnel entrance less than twenty strides from where the midnight visitor had come down past the sheer east wall.

The tunnel entrance was pretty well silted up. Since Sammy Darling with his rifle was posted outside the arroyo on a promontory overlooking all approaches, Johnston, predictably, was elected to man the shovel.

It didn't take him long to gain them access and the preliminary inspection occupied but half an hour. The tunnel, cluttered with loose rock, went straight in for about sixty feet, then turned at right angles to strike south for twenty more, at which point it terminated in a ladder-hung shaft.

The walls were clammy with moisture. The air smelled foul. McCready, holding the torch out to light up the hole, said, "Go ahead," to Oberbit. "We had better find out how high that water's standing."

Oberbit slewed him an irritable look. He got down on his hunkers and studied the ladder without much enthusiasm. Peering over the edge he caught a look at his reflection. He saw the girl's face, too — she looked excited and nervous.

He got up and stepped back until his shoulder brushed a wall. "It stands within ten feet of us right now. If you ain't satisfied with a guess climb down an' measure it yourself."

McCready peered at the ladder. It was a primitive affair constructed of two peeled poles with crosspieces at sixteen inch intervals, these lashed with thongs cut from horse- or cowhide which, from long immersion, likely would not hold anything heavier than a frog.

The lawyer said, "Can you judge what kind of pump we'll need?"

"Close enough," Johnston said. "I doubt if you'll find one nearer than 'Frisco. Even then it'll have to be packed in from

194

Phoenix. From what I've seen so far it looks to cost a lot more than you will ever git out of it."

McCready told the girl, "That's enthusiasm for you."

The girl put her hand on Johnston's arm and could feel the temper quivering inside him. "What's the matter?" she said.

Still eyeing the fat man, Oberbit grumbled, "You want the plain truth? I don't think a pump is like to make much difference. I think this mine's played out — or worked out."

Into the shocked silence McCready said smoothly, "The kind of remark I'd expect from a man who would spend ten years chasing the tail of a mule. He wouldn't recognize the real thing if it fell down on top of him," he told Micaela with a snort of contempt. "We know that from what he did with the two mines he located. Why, you've only to look at the walls of this cut to know this claim is a real bonanza — you can see blue quartz wherever you look."

Johnston said with curled lip, "What you're lookin' at *is* quartz. Blue quartz, sure; you don't see any gold though . . . not enough to matter. Them Peraltas weren't fools. The reason none of 'em ever came back is because there wasn't nothin' left to come back to!"

The girl, bewildered, looked from one to the other.

"All right," McCready said, "if you really believe what you're preaching I'll take that half interest off your hands. I'll even pay enough boot to see you out of here."

Johnston reached for the paper in his pocket but, seeing the girl's face, brought the hand out empty. "You see?" McCready smiled. "When the chips are down it's a different story."

Johnston, appearing still of two minds, fetched the short-handled prospector's pick from his belt and began tapping walls. He broke off several pieces, let them go with disgust. He peered at the rubble that lay underfoot. "Let's have some light on this." He picked up several chunks of rock from the roof, rubbed them clean and, scowling, threw back his head to study for a moment the holes they'd dropped out of. Handing one of the pieces to Micaela he discarded the others and looked again at the dripping walls.

"What's that?" asked the fat man, eyeing the chunk Micaela was holding; and Oberbit, moving toward the right-angle turn that led to the entrance, growled,

"Just somethin' to remember this hole in the ground by. We could probably scrape up maybe three, four thousand bucks' worth if we worked at it hard enough, but them quitclaims this razzledazzler's been peddlin' the suckers will build a stake a helluva lot quicker."

"Right out of the horse's mouth," sighed the lawyer. "As a short-change artist of no mean repute he's certainly qualified to speak on anything relating to hoodwinking suckers." He took a fresh breath to say with bright malice, "If there's anyone around this neck of the woods who has gone through more of other folks' money —"

"Oh, stop it!" Micaela cried, distraught. "Name calling isn't going to solve anything! If it's as bad as he says —"

"But it's not. He doesn't know what is at the bottom of that shaft. We'll need a pump to find out, and by the fact that, contrary to orders, he conveniently forgot to send for one inclines me to suspect he's got an educated hunch.

"This feller's not the ignorant numbskull he's managed to make folks think. I had him thoroughly looked into before I consented to let you engage him, Micaela; he's a working geologist who's been through the School of Mines at Golden, Colorado."

He looked around at Johnston coolly. "He knows the kind of terrain, the sort of formations, which favor the production of what we're looking for." He said very earnestly, "When you're dealing with a man who has no regard for scruples you should take anything he tells you with a pinch or two of salt."

Peering into her eyes he said, "When have I misled you? I have every confidence in the worth of this mine. One thing he said I'm compelled to agree with: the Peraltas were not fools. They'd not have kept this map if the mine was worked out; no man could have played a prank of such cruelty on the blood of his blood, the children's children he'd expect to come after him. This is the treasure he would put aside for them, the hope of some distant rainy day.

"Johnston tells you this mine is played out. I can tell you what is in the back of his mind. If you allow him to pull the wool over your eyes and insist on abandoning it you may be sure he'll come back, once we've cleared out, and make himself a fortune because of your credulity."

The girl's round eyes looked doubtfully after Oberbit who, with the tool put back in his belt, had picked his way over the fallen rubble and was rounding the turn that led out of the tunnel. "I can't believe he would do such a thing."

"Of course you can't," McCready said gravely. "Your mind is conditioned by the cloistered surroundings in which you grew up. You've had no experience of the world as it is, the dog-eat-dog tactics by which men like Johnston get ahead of their fellows to reach whatever goal they've set their mark on. You find him different, perhaps exciting; in your thoughts you have built him into something he would laugh at, some kind of modern knight, selflessly devoted —"

She said, a little crossly, "What do you want of me?"

"Only the chance to prove I am right. Your consent to go ahead with this and pile up the fortune I know this mine is capable of producing."

XXV

Johnston didn't catch more than half of that conversation but he reckoned from what he'd heard that McCready would have his way in the matter. Micaela's inexperience and dependence on the lawyer were matters no amount of argument would change. The man's *purpose* was something else altogether.

It was the fat man who had named this hole the 'lost' Salvation, a mind-filling phrase, suggestive and provocative. Something you could sell to the gullible and greedy. As McCready had so snidely pointed out, Oberbit was one who understood such advantages and had some history in making the most of them. He could guess pretty shrewdly which direction the dude was bound for.

The lawyer aimed to build this up to where he could peddle it — that much was plain. With his kind of assurance it could run to five figures if he was left to develop his hoax unimpeded.

From the elbow turn he called out to Johnston and Oberbit wheeled, half minded to say what was on his mind. He was riled enough but better judgment prevailed, for what could he say that would not make him either look silly or like a back-biting ingrate in the girl's eyes? McCready held all the cards.

He came up in his muddy yellow shoes with the diamond glistening in his ascot tie and the derby cockily a-tilt above eyes smugly shining with saturnine amusement. "I was wondering if, from the loftiness of your experienced opinion, you would point out to my ignorance the difference here between quartz with gold in it and the kind you call worthless?" Including Micaela, the fat man said, "We'd both like to know."

Oberbit looked at the chunks the dude held. He turned over a couple, growled, "Plain junk," and tossed them away. But the next one he took from McCready's hand he considered with narrowing, wondering eyes. It was larger, even better, than the one — confiscated by Weminuche — the girl had given him. "This one," he grumbled, "is what they call 'jewelry rock' — see all them flecks, them oblong crystals? Looks like iron pyrites or Sylvanite, kind of. When this piece is roasted you'll have a button of pure gold." He considered, looking thoughtful. "Where'd you find it?"

"I picked all of them up off the floor back there," the lawyer said smugly, retrieving his specimen. "Well, don't let me keep you."

The girl followed Oberbit out of the tunnel. "Has that changed your mind?"

Johnston shook his head. "I stick with what I told you before. If there was enough here to bother with, them Peraltas wouldn't've left it settin' all this time. When this mine was being worked the ore, I would imagine, was fetched up in baskets by Indian labor. What your fat friend found was a piece that was dropped. Like enough he'll find others, but a handful of highgrade don't make a mine, without you're lookin' to salt one. Which he probably is."

"Salt?"

"That's what they call it when someone takes a worthless hole and pretties it up with a sackful of highgrade — ore that shows gold in bonanza quantity."

She said a little shocked, "You think Dan would — ?"

"I think he'd do anything if there was enough profit in it." He regarded her sourly. "When you goin' to wake up, for Chrissake? You're the mouth-wateringest meal ticket he's ever got hold of!"

"Oh!" she cried and, head high, departed in a riled swish of skirts.

An hour or so later, while Oberbit was moving his picketed mule, McCready emerged from the tunnel with pockets bulging and arms filled with rocks. Depositing these beside the fire's burnt-out ashes, he took a long look around and came across to say brusquely, "Mind if I borrow that pickhammer of yours?"

Seeing nothing to be gained by refusing, Oberbit passed it over. No need to ask what the dude aimed to do with it. Any fool could see he meant to break up his samples. "Looks like you're fixin' to get ready for business."

McCready, smiling coolly, went off to get at it.

Breaking them up would make them go farther and give an appearance of freshness advantageous to his intention.

A short while later as Johnston, building up the fire, was sorting through the tinned stuffs and staples they had got from Jubal Clee, a racket of hoof sound and clattering wheels announced the arrival of the three teams from Sunflower highpiled with lumber and other things he'd paid the storekeeper to have driven out here.

The hostler who'd claimed to be able to run lines was beside the driver on the lead wagon's seat, and a passenger likewise rode each of the others — probably the carpenters McCready had ordered.

Johnston, straightening, waved and they cut around toward his fire.

McCready left off what he was doing to come over, pompously important, glance swiveling over the loads. Dusting off his hands with Irish linen, he said to the nearest driver, "At ten dollars a day I can use about three more hands around here."

Oberbit figured he had them right then but the fellow, eyes bright with curiosity, asked, "What's up?" with the rest of the townsmen leaning forward to hear.

The lawyer beamed like he was little Jack Horner. "We're about to reopen the lost Salvation mine," he said, and waddled over to hand up to each driver a fist-sized piece from his collection of ore samples.

There was no doubt in Johnston that the word would get around and lose nothing in the telling. You had only to see those bugged eyes and dropped jaws.

The driver sitting next to the hostler cried hoarsely, "What the hell *is* this?"

McCready smiled. "That, my friend, is tellurium. According to our mining expert," he said with an acknowledging half amused glance at a glowering Oberbit, "a telluride of gold that will probably assay about fifteen or twenty thousand dollars to the ton."

Oh, he was cute, all right, palming off Johnston as authority for his outrageous statement, coolly defying Oberbit to deny it, knowing people would believe what they wanted to believe and that any retraction he might now attempt would serve only to convince them he was trying to cover up a cat let prematurely out of the bag.

Their avid stares took in his resentment and two of the drivers, jumping off their wagons, came forward with an eagerness as preposterous as their credulity. "You've got me hired right now," said the first, and "You kin put my name in the book," cried the other; "Ossie Hampton, a damn good man to have in your corner!"

The other driver, with a wistful scowl, resisted the contagion and stayed with his wagon, though it was plain he was tempted and sorely reluctant to stay with a job that was taking him nowhere.

McCready put his two new recruits to the work of unloading and, drawing Oberbit aside, said with lowered voice, "You'd better stake out the discovery claim straightaway and another for Weminuche — we got to keep that feller amenable. But the number one extension you'll record in my name, and I guess you had better stake one for Sammy. When you're through get on your mule and make a beeline for the county seat."

"You mean," Johnston sneered, "you'll be satisfied with one? I kinda figured a man of your enterprise would sew up the whole east side of this gulch!"

The fat man grinned. "Just do as I tell you — I'll have what I want. You have to think big in a game of this kind; it's the overall picture, not the right now that matters. Finesse, my boy, is the thing that builds bridges."

Oberbit said, "An' what about that pair you just hired on? You think they're going to stand twiddlin' their thumbs —"

"I always take care of a friend . . . or an enemy. They'll get their chance to stake a good claim. You can record them with ours. We'll let them pick out a site soon's you get the rest rocked."

"And what's to prevent them from plastering the gulch?"

McCready put a hand on his shoulder and pointed at Darling, standing up there against the sky with his rifle. "That answer your question?" He slapped the shoulder affectionately. "I think you'll find I've got an answer for everything — and that includes you. Don't forget when you're up at the county seat to send for that pump. We've got to make this look good."

He pushed Oberbit away, strode off to put the carpenters to work at their jobs.

Bemused though disgruntled, Johnston got down to the business of staking out claims as per the fat man's instructions. He was tired of his own cooking anyway and could get a square meal when he got to town. He gathered up some empty cans to put his notices in, ambled down into the arroyo and headed for the tunnel mouth to start counting off the feet.

But those tracks in the mud where boots had crossed last night jogged him away from the treadmill groove of his frustrating conclusions. Concerned as McCready was with his own crooked schemes perhaps the fat dude wasn't sharp as he thought.

No matter how you sliced it there was some kind of deal — consummated or at least in the wind — between this cow bunch and Weminuche, and Oberbit nervously thought it unlikely the fat man's hardnosed remarks to Clee would hold off whatever they had hatched up for long.

About the only thing to give a man solace was the unstable conviction that, glass or no glass and try as they might, nobody — without they came down here to look — could possibly know what he wrote on these notices.

XXVI

No matter how practical a man's habit of looking at things, most people occasionally find themselves toying with fanciful daydreams and Oberbit Johnston, coming back from the county seat aboard his gray mule, was gloomily engrossed in the saddest dreams of all — those which he knew were already turned to ashes.

He must have been crazy anyway to imagine there could ever have been anything between them — a girl like her brought up as she had been, daughter of a don, descendent of a baron, with all of Guadalajara probably at her feet.

Those glances he'd intercepted, the electric touch of her hand, though spurring his pulse to headlong gallop and reducing his legs to the quiver of reeds, had likely meant no more to Micaela than finding weevils in the biscuits would to that rusty-faced Sammy. It was over now anyway, irreparably scuttled when by implication he'd labeled McCready a scheming swindler and herself a deluded fool.

He'd sometimes found it hard, surreptitiously considering her, to keep his mind on scraping up a stake, which was all he'd ever come out here for. He wouldn't need to remind himself of *that* anymore!

A mighty thin satisfaction. About on a par with his stubborn refusal to order a pump he was bitterly convinced no one would have any use for. If things worked out as McCready expected, that highbinder would be long gone with bulging pockets before any machinery could get here.

In a grudging sort of fashion you had to kind of admire the slippery slickness, the cunning ingenuity, with which the fat rascal was going about this. From the start it had taken a real sharp spider to weave a workable web from such sleight of hand illusions when one instant's carelessness, a single false step, could bring the whole shimmering structure collapsing about his ears in a roar of retribution. Guys like Clee and Weminuche Bill just weren't the sort to stamp your boot and yell *Boo!* at.

At the fat dude's insistence, Oberbit had fetched along a sack of samples he'd dropped off at an assayer's — not that McCready really cared two hoots whether he got a report. Just another instance of razzle dazzle intended to show values he felt sure the assayer would be too excited to keep to himself.

McCready wanted a rush, had everything geared to it, and Johnston reckoned he would like enough get one; and yet two things about this deal still were capable of considerably surprising him — the speed and ramifications of McCready's maneuvering.

He got the first of these jolts when, crossing the final spur above the encampment where he'd left the lawyer and his just-arrived teams, he spied a fresh put-up sign whose letters, burned into white pine with a cinch ring, read: SALVATION — 1 MILE AHEAD.

But his astonishment at this was as nothing compared to the open-mouth, breath-snatched, goggling incredulity which came over him some yards later when he got his first look at the scene below: the whole of that bench to the south of the lake bed was crammed and bustling with activity and people.

There must have been half a hundred men scampering about. At least twenty tents had gone up beyond Micaela's. The whole arroyo throbbed with comings and goings and that east rim slope appeared acrawl with figures scurrying like ants from a burning log.

Staring like a ninny, Johnston felt light-headed. He thought first off his eyes were playing him tricks; he even went so far as to pinch himself in the thought he might be dreaming. But it was all real enough. He hadn't missed the trail and wound up someplace else because there, just north of the cracked mud in that arroyo, were the pens and buildings of Jubal Clee's Roman Five.

In the midst of the tents a wooden shack had gone up, testifying to the industry of McCready's importations, a queue of joggling, impatient men standing querulously grumbling before its door. Johnston, putting his mule down the ridge's far side, aimed its rolling gait toward the twelve foot sign which announced in bold flourish: SALVATION TOWNSITE HEADQUARTERS — *Dan McCready, Mayor Pro Tem.*

Stepping down by the door, shoving men off his elbows, he went into the shack like he couldn't get there fast enough, yet knew straightaway he was hours too late.

At a knocked-together unvarnished desk McCready sat in all his charm behind two stacks of printed forms parting fools from their cash smooth as a combine removing grain from stems and chaff. With a grin and a slap he sped them along, some with one paper, others with two, each hailed like a long lost friend.

One sharp swiveling glance was more than plenty. Town lots and mining stock, neither worth enough to gag a half dead flea — stuff he must have had printed in Mexico.

Those mining certificates were real works of art. They looked good as hard money, bright with colored inks and engraving, garnished with curlicues, spread eagles and gold sacks. But the come-on, stacked right in plain sight between pen and pistol, was well nigh irresistible — that blue glistening mound of tellurium samples, jewelry rock every piece of it.

"Oh, there you are!" McCready cried, looking up as Johnston, glowering, dropped anchor beside him. "Our mining expert, gentlemen, Mr. Oberbit Johnston, celebrated discoverer of the Silver King and the great Bull Weevil. He's the feller you've got to thank for relocating that pride of the Peraltas, the lost Salvation, and sparking a strike that's going to open up — and may very well prove to be — one of the richest districts in the all-time history of American mining!"

With those gullible fools setting up a cheer, Oberbit, strangling a bitter curse, stomped out of the place like a man looking around for a hound to kick. Latching onto his mule he slammed into the saddle and with face black as thunder hurled him into the arroyo, bound in a fury for the Salvation tunnel mouth.

What he expected from this wasn't clear even to him. He was too worked up to stand around and keep still — yet what could he say? Half of them, even if told the truth, would refuse to believe it, and the other half — those that might stop to listen — would be outraged enough to string up the whole push, himself included . . . maybe even Micaela.

He'd seen mobs work before. With shivery remembrance he allowed Tallow Eye to drop out of his gallop, gradually taking in the activity around him. The lake bed was rocked in every direction, men with rifles standing over their notices like they figured he might be intending to jump them!

Then, peering against the sunglare ahead, he spotted the shack built of new whip-sawed pine that completely concealed the hole he was bound for. Another of McCready's signs was nailed across it just above the opened door in which Darling sat astride a crate with his rifle. When near enough to read it, Johnston cursed. It said: SALVATION MINE — *No Admittance.* Under this: OBERBIT JOHNSTON, MICAELA PERALTA, OWNERS.

Sammy showed his sour grin when Johnston pulled up. "Hello, owner," he hailed with a guffaw. "Guess you can see we've carried out your orders. Some of them boys thought it kind of harsh you wouldn't let 'em in for a look till I told 'em how bothered you'd been with samplin', guys carryin' off all the highgrade in sight. Somethin' on your mind, boss?"

Hearing steps back of him Johnston flung around to find half a dozen curious claim stakers eyeing him, among them Ossie Hampton, one of the two drivers McCready had hired away from the Sunflower Mercantile.

"When you people figure to start producin'?" Hampton asked, touching his hat. "Some of us here would like to get a little work to kind of tide us over . . ."

Before Oberbit could put his foot into it the rusty-faced Darling spoke up to say gruffly, "We got no end of jobs but no time fer loafers. Like you know, this whole gulch has been under water; we can't do much inside till the pumps git here to clear the shaft."

He considered them dubiously. "Expect we could find work fer picks an' shovels if you wanta scrape up a little eatin' money."

He said in an aside to Johnston, "You been talkin' about a hoist connection. You wanta go up with 'em, boss, and show this bunch where to put down the hole?"

Oberbit had never said a word about a hoist so the whole idea must have come from McCready, but it plainly made sense to connect shaft with surface if the mine was ever to go into production. This bunch would expect it. It was a cheap way of keeping them happy for a spell. That son of a bitch didn't miss a bet.

"All right," he said, "we'll want it ten foot across. We can use four of you diggin' in shifts. Who wants in?"

Hampton said, "I'll take a whack at it." The long-nosed one nodded and two others without very noticeable enthusiasm signified their willingness to at least have a look at it. Oberbit said to Hampton, "Thought you had a job with McCready?"

"I helped put up this an' the townsite shack."

"Didn't he have nothin' else for you?"

"I didn't hear him mention it."

"All right. Get your tools," Johnston said, "an' I'll meet you up top."

"Now that's what I like about you." Darling grinned as the others moved to fetch picks and shovels. "You're quick to see where your best interests lie. Real adaptable," he said with a snicker.

Oberbit's vexation was beginning to assume a rather perilous complexion not at all soothed by having to absorb such venom-tipped barbs from a ranny he despised as heartily as this one. But he got into his saddle, smiling with his teeth while he tried with deeper breath to hold back the bile that was threatening to choke him.

"Oh, by the way," Sammy said like it was something he'd just remembered, "your friend Weminuche stopped by a couple hours ago. Seemed downright anxious to bend a few words with you."

Johnston, twisting in his saddle like a scorpion had got up his pantsleg, banged both heels into the ribs of his startled mount and sent Tallow Eye in a boil of dust up the acclivitous trail that snaked around toward the rim above the tunnel's shack-hid entrance.

He didn't need to consult any crystal ball to be sure his health would stay in much better shape if he never ran into Weminuche again. This was too much to hope for with that hardnosed plug-ugly wanting to know where his claim was, but the longer such a meeting could be postponed the better Oberbit would like it. That feller had a temper it didn't bear to think about.

After Johnston had rimmed out up on the bench he looked nervously about with the wind cuffing his hat and tugging at his vest flaps. Mindful of the glass Weminuche had mentioned he felt about as prominent as a boil on a pugged nose. The monuments of new-staked claims abounded here in bewildering profusion but he did not observe anything imminently alarming.

Over there, off beyond the hodgepodge of tents, three or four figures were still in line at the townsite shack waiting their turn to augment McCready's stake; he picked out Micaela's skirted shape bound on some errand in the arroyo's direction, recalled how it had felt with her pressed hard against him that time she had reached up to give him a kiss.

Unconsciously scowling, he noticed a group in gesticulating argument outside the opened flap of the largest tent, and here and yon among the studding of monuments an occasional man plying pick or shovel in the fruitless hope of uncovering ore.

He might, of course, be wrong in considering such labor to be of no avail. Although the terrain around here, geologically speaking, seemed hardly conducive to mineralization on any scale fit for mining, the Peraltas, at least, appeared to have struck paydirt. But the vein had pinched out — he felt as confident of that as a man could well be. It was the only likelihood a feller would dare bank on, for what man in his senses would abandon a mine that still held rock half as good as that sample Micaela had given him?

The hired four arrived puffing and sweating from their arduous climb, and Oberbit, not relinquishing his seat aboard the gray mule, blandly pointed out where they should dig — not that it made any great amount of difference whether they missed the shaft by a matter of inches or as much as ten feet. A gallowsframe and hoist would probably do as much good if they stuck them like a steeple on the townsite shack!

Picking up his reins, "Remember," he growled at Hampton, "no blasting. We can't chance a cave-in with this ground like it is."

"How far you figure we're goin' to have to go?"

Oberbit shrugged. "Fifty, sixty feet, I'd say. That timberin' down there's pretty well shot. I expect," he told them grimly, "you'd better quit an' climb out when you're down to a twelve foot leeway. That shaft, if you fell into it, could damn well be the last thing you'd see."

He rode off toward the tents. They'd have to take time tomorrow to rig up a winch. Probably be three or four days before they got into any ground that was dangerous. He'd speak to McCready about retimbering that tunnel and then, if there was any necessity for carrying this farce further, they could put in some sets and push on up from below. If that fat son was half as smart as he appeared he'd take his profit and clear out before this hoax blew up in his face.

Still and all, a feller couldn't help worrying with a vinegarroon like that damned Weminuche camping on his shirttail — not to mention Clee and his cow wallopers setting back there like Apaches nursing up their hate.

XXVII

The hostler who doubled for surveyor had departed now that the Salvation town lots had been laid out. That was one thing about McCready — once your usefulness was ended he sure didn't keep a man standing about.

In spite of Oberbit's convictions the fat man's suavely confident mien was like a contagion. The tone of the camp, if not its whole outlook, became noticeably cheerful with new faces coming in every hour, by foot and horseback, in spring wagons, buggies and buckboards. The rough tracks over which McCready's lumber had been fetched had been beaten into a dust-fogged well-traveled road, and now there was talk of running a stage.

Scarcely a week had slipped past since the lawyer had put town lots on the market, yet that hodgepodge of flung-up tents had already become part of a street sporting six saloons, a bake shop, mercantile, pool hall and gunsmith's. With no ore in sight except for McCready's much-circulated samples, men were at work on more than half the claims, at least twenty had changed hands for fat lump sums and the camp's population had reached almost a thousand, with new structures rising all over the flats.

There was talk of a smelter and there were round-the-clock guards at the Salvation's tunnel shack. It was rumored the tunnel had been retimbered under Johnston's direction; a gallowsframe rose above the hole being dug to connect with the old working's water-filled shaft, and hoist machinery stood in labeled crates outside the mercantile.

Every bar was crowded and George Graham Rice, the Wall Street operator, had come down from Goldfield. Tex Rickard was in town and talking about opening up another Great Northern. Rice had bought a block of six claims for — it was said — fifty thousand dollars and was spending considerable time in Dan McCready's company. H. W. Knickerbocker was going to open a reduction mill, and High-Step Gertie arrived with her girls.

To all of which Oberbit could only shake his head. McCready seemed adroitly to be keeping out of his way, too busy with his gold-plated miracle to have any time for footless conversations. He was alleged to be fuming with impatience over the failure of the pumps he had ordered to materialize, but he did not seek out Johnston for an accounting.

And then, on a morning that seemed no different from any other, Oberbit, about to step into the Big Horn Bar, came face to face with his old friend Weminuche, whose expression lit up in a wicked grin.

"Gotcha!" he grated, and caught Oberbit's arm in a grip like a vise. "Come on, chum, we got some talkin' to unravel!"

Victim of his most dreaded nightmare, Oberbit's stare jumped around like a boxful of crickets without finding anything that looked like help. At this ungainly hour traffic was almost nonexistent, and the few perambulating shapes he glimpsed were too far away and too wrapped up in their own perplexities to spare any interest for other folks' problems.

Propelled down an alley through a clutter of trash, throat too dry and thoughts too chaotic to produce anything more coherent than splutters, Johnston found his back against a wall, pinned in place by a ham-like fist.

"Start yappin'!"

Gulping, goggling, Oberbit's stare was observably miserable.

With curling lip but no easement of glower, the highgrader rasped, "You been around long enough to know what kin happen to any sidewindin' shorthorn that goes outa his way to cross up a feller that figured him a buddy!"

"Fer God's sake, Bill —"

"Don't 'Bill' me, you friggin' two-by-four welcher!" Weminuche's eyes were glittering pools of unwinking malevolence, his thrust-forward chin a scant half inch from Oberbit's nose. "I just got back from the county seat!"

Johnston guessed, copiously sweating, this murderous mood to have been inspired by a look at the record books. "Wh— what you want me to do?"

"I'll tell you once an' you'll do it right quick if you don't want them legs folded over a crate-top an' buzzards waitin' to git at your eyes."

He took a fresh grip that ground Johnston's shoulderblades against the rough wall. "I want that paper the Peralta filly give you an' I want it signed over to me — *right now!*"

This was so unexpected that Oberbit, rather light-headed by this respite from dire peril, thought the shake in his knees must surely unhinge them. To cover this embarrassment he cried in half strangled bluster, "You expect me to write it in blood with my finger?"

"There's a pen on that table in McCready's office. We'll go over there — an' no tricks, by God, or you'll never make it!"

Ossie Hampton stood lounging with his back to the saloon front as Johnston, prodded by his captor, emerged from the alley. Oberbit, too bemused to notice, stumbled past without seeing him, but Weminuche gave the ex-teamster a hard, sharp-eyed stare before following the prospector on up the street.

No men were queued at the townsite door, it being scarcely eight o'clock and still faintly cool from the night's lowered temperatures, but the fat man was back of his table-desk inside, apparently busy toting up a list of figures, which he forsook with irritation when Weminuche came shoving Johnston toward him.

"What do you want?" he demanded gruffly, an unreadable stare appraising Johnston's flushed face before swiveling to Weminuche.

"Goodie Two Boots here has got some

writin' to take care of. Thought perhaps he might borrer your scratcher there."

McCready, looking again at Oberbit's odd expression, said, "How much writing? How long's it going to take?"

"Won't take but a minute," Weminuche said with a mean kind of grin.

The lawyer shoved his pen across the boards.

"Shake it up, sport," Weminuche, nudging Oberbit, growled.

Since the prospector seemed convinced the Salvation was worthless, anyone in the know might be hard pressed to understand his indecision. Half a share of nothing was still bound to be nothing. Why this reluctance to put pen to paper?

Was it just that he hated to think of Micaela saddled with this conscienceless ruffian? Or was there back of his fidgeting nervousness some hidden sharp edge of more personal reason?

With a disgruntled sigh he dug from a pocket the much folded paper McCready had given him. Even before he got it all the way open it was plain the fat slob had grasped what was coming.

He half rose from his chair, blanched cheeks quivering, agitated eyes sweeping Oberbit's face. "You're not trading your half to this joker, are you?" Voice climbing with apprehension, he reached for his wallet. "If you want out of this, Johnston, I'll —"

"He's already out," Weminuche informed him. "Set back an' keep those paws plenty still!" He stood over him like a hulking buzzard till the lawyer put both hands on the table, then grinned with an evident relish. "Your lah-de-dah ward's got a new partner, fatso — one which knows how to look out for her interests.

"Grab up that pen, chum," he rasped with his stare never leaving McCready, "an' don't try to play me for no sucker again! Write this: 'For one dollar and other valuable considerations I, Oberbit Johnston, do hereby bargain, sell, convey and confirm unto Weminuche Bill Baylor, his heirs and assigns forever, all rights, shares and interest given me by this document.' "

McCready, face glistening, cried in a wild, half strangled voice, "That thing's not binding —"

"It'll bind all right 'fore I git done with it," Weminuche assured him, peering across Johnston's shoulder. "Sign it."

Oberbit signed.

"Your turn, fatso." The highgrader

grinned across the snout of a pistol. "Write: 'Dan McCready, attorney at law, witness and guardian.' Now put the date on it. . . . Obliged, gents." He chuckled, picking up the paper, waving it a moment before stuffing it inside his shirtfront. "Don't know when I've had a more pleasurable mornin'."

He backed toward the door, feeling behind him for the latch.

"You'll not get away with this!" the lawyer grated.

Weminuche laughed. He said to Oberbit, "I'm off to the county seat to record this. When I come back I'll be fetchin' a preacher along with a license. We'll have us a weddin' this camp can date time by." He looked hard at McCready. "Don't git in my way or you'll have Roman Five ridin' through this camp like the wrath of God."

XXVIII

No sooner had the sound of his steps died away than McCready burst out from the midst of his fluster. "Is that feller off his nut?"

Oberbit lugubriously shook his head.

He'd had a hunch all the time Weminuche was bad medicine but he had sure never looked for tidings like these — and the worst of it was the bastard meant every bit of it. Whoever he'd drummed up in Tombstone to help him could be ensconced right now in this camp, keeping cases, ready to strike at the first breach of hostility.

"But the girl's not of age! He can't force her into —"

"He can try like hell if he's made up his mind to it," Oberbit snarled, kicking a chair half across the room. "He don't give a damn whether school keeps or not an' there's no law nearer'n the county seat. This bugger buffaloed the Mountain Maid management straight into bankruptcy; you think a fat-ass shyster's goin' to scare him off? He's had a look at the records an' knows every claim I went up there to put on the books is down in the name of Micaela Peralta."

Shock washed across that derby-hatted face, all the lines of it twisting into a crumple of dismay, the last vestige of color departing the plump cheeks as the lawyer thrust a bracing hand toward the wall.

"We got no time for hysterics," Johnston growled. "Pull yourself together! We got just one chance to keep him off that girl."

McCready, stiffening, found a stump of cigar, put a match to it, savagely puffing while bitter eyes raked Oberbit with the unveiled promise of a dire hereafter.

Johnston said, "He's got to be shown that mine's a dud."

The fat man swelled like a bloating toad. "If you think I'm going to buy that you're crazy!" Eyes bright with spleen he hammered the words like shot from a Gatling: "You get down to that tunnel shack and send Darling up here! On the double — you hear? Meanwhile no one's to go in there — nobody! Get going!"

After Sammy took off, Oberbit gloomily sat down in the doorway, miserably wishing he'd thought to fetch his bottle.

He couldn't see any way out of this impasse other than the obvious one he'd suggested, unless McCready was able to get the man killed. That he intended to try seemed to go without saying — why else would he have sent for the gunfighter?

Weminuche doubtless expected him to try. Be a short horse soon curried. Darling hadn't the chance of a snowball in hell. Hadn't Johnston himself once disarmed that poor fool? Fellers like him Bill could eat before breakfast — and several times had.

Still . . .

McCready, Johnston remembered, was not altogether helpless. He likely had more than one string to his bow and, if past performance was any criterion, there was a pretty fair chance he'd come out on top yet.

Micaela was the one a man had to feel sorry for. She stood to lose either way. He had thought by recording all those claims in her name that if there was any rock here worth the trouble of mining she would wind up with most of the trumps in her hand.

But he'd forgotten one thing: like the fat man had said, she was still under age. All of her affairs were in McCready's hands;

she couldn't, independently, scarcely blow her nose without that son of a bitch's permission!

Was the pen really mightier than the sword?

The lawyer had shown himself slicker than slobbers but Weminuche was a past master at cutting red tape with the bark of a pistol. In Tombstone violence had been his stock answer to everything and he had come out on top, no doubt about that. No question but his intention was to do so again.

He'd have Clee and his Roman Five crew pulling for him. McCready had caught Roman Five with its pants down but with Weminuche in the saddle and calling the shots that hardcased crew could be a different breed of cats. And he had other things going for him, like this anonymous help he'd fetched from Tombstone that nobody here could put a finger on.

Known men you might deal with, but how to fight phantoms?

Those fellers could be anywhere — anyone. Even in Tombstone some of Bill's bunch had never been uncovered, free to get in their licks and exact reprisals against anyone brash enough to stand against him.

The frustrated whirl of Oberbit's thinking abruptly pulled Hampton out of his head.

And he thought, eyes scrinched almost shut, *Why not?* The jasper could be one of them, infiltrated into the mercantile's employ to meet the unexpected demands of Johnston's three-wagon order, insinuated into this Salvation setup as driver of one of those loads sent over.

When McCready had made his ten dollar offer hadn't Hampton been the first to accept? Oberbit remembered him jumping off the wagon: "Ossie Hampton," he'd said; "a damn good man to have in your corner." He'd been available, too, when they'd wanted that hole dug.

Why had McCready dispensed with his services?

And with the street practically deserted he'd been lounging against the front of that grog shop when Weminuche had prodded Johnston out of that alley. . . .

Still again — after the highgrader's chuckling departure — when Oberbit had left McCready just now to summon Sammy Darling, Hampton was sunning himself against the side of the shack, hunkered on his bootheels whittling a stick.

Coincidence?

Johnston snorted. All who believed that could stand on their heads!

He peered around worriedly. This was

like to get worse before it got any better. Right now he couldn't see any way out, but he had to keep trying. It was unthinkable that Micaela should be whipsawed like this. There must be something a man could do to help her.

If there was he couldn't seem to get his hooks into it.

Half an hour later — still wrestling with the problem — horse sound mingled with approaching boot steps pulled the chin off his chest to find Darling headed horseback toward him alongside Hampton, who was lugging a rifle.

It was the gunfighter first that caught and held Oberbit's notice — the middle of him mostly, that bright and shiny bit of tin cut in the shape of a marshal's star that winked from the swing of the pistolero's open coat.

With knee around the horn and a twisted grin Sammy said, "Law has come to Salvation, Johnston," and stuck out his chest like a feisty bantam. "From here on out folks had better step careful, them anyways that aim to keep walkin'."

Hampton stood poker-still waiting on his pleasure. Johnston, scalp prickling, said, "What's this jigger doin' here?"

"We're puttin' on extry men, what else? Ossie here's been made chief of our mine guards. We've got one posted on each of them claims you so finely filed for Micaela Peralta, just to make sure no wildcatter jumps 'em. Ossie'll take over here — you're to come with me. The fat boy's got other plans fer you, bucko."

Johnston, staring slit-eyed at his replacement, said, "But God damn it —"

"No buts, sport. C'mon, let's git whackin'."

Mouth still crammed with his unspoken protests, Oberbit scowlingly let himself be herded off across the noisy length of the arroyo up onto the bench and into the crush of the camp's single street, ajar with a midmorning traffic of shouting pedestrians, spur-jingling horsebackers and the rattle-bang clatter of sundry wagons, whose principal contribution apparently was the production and stirring of prodigious amounts of well-nigh strangling flour-like dust.

Newcomers abounded wherever one looked and a straggling line of impatient, gesticulating, loud talking strangers once again was queued up before McCready's closed door.

Breasting these suckers, coming up to the head of them, the gangling Sammy dropped out of his saddle and impervious to grumblings, shoving Oberbit ahead of him, pushed open the door, heeling it shut in one swearing man's face.

Been time enough coming up here for Johnston to decide this perhaps wasn't the moment to kick over the traces with unprovable suspicions, but he did think the lawyer ought to be alerted. "Before you start giving out like Caesar, I want," he said, "to bring up these rannies you've put on for mine guards. Ain't it struck you maybe some of them could be Weminuche's pals?"

Plainly it hadn't by McCready's expression. He chewed on his lip, then waved it away with an irascible snort. "That's Darling's department. I want you to —"

"I'm through runnin' errands," Oberbit growled. "I want some straight talk. You've said often enough that girl's in your hands. How far you figure to go to protect her?"

Sammy said meanly, "You want I should pop him?"

McCready looked out of dark cheeks to say thinly, "I've a good thing here. I'm not about to be shook loose of it."

Oberbit nodded. "That's good enough for me. From here on, mister, you can skin your own rabbits."

"Hold on! Where you off to?"

"I'm makin' Micaela my *personal* responsibility."

XXIX

After quitting McCready and his newly made marshal, Oberbit, stuffed with the heady satisfactions of virtue, set off up the street like he was lord of the mountains. This bright and refreshing sense of euphoria lasted about as far as a pimp could swing a ten pound hammer, at which point the sight of four Roman Five horses racked at a tie rail fronting the Pink Elephant conjured nasty remembrances of Weminuche Bill.

He had thought to stop by and have a chat with Micaela but a sudden dryness of throat chased him into a bar, where a good stiff belt seemed to call for another and found him, several drinks later, hunched over a bottle at a back corner table.

He'd made some pretty windy boasts in his time but when he'd told that fat shyster he'd take care of the girl he had meant every dadburned word of it. Lofty words and subsequent performance do not in this world always go hand in hand and he could not for the life of him, looking at it now, see the remotest possibility of making that brag stand up.

He couldn't understand why he'd been fool enough to make it. Things were so turned around in his head he reckoned he scarcely knew up from down. One thing, though, he could plainly see. A guy would have more luck crawling empty-handed into a bear's den than squaring off to tangle with the likes of Weminuche. You had maybe two chances of coming out on top: grab the girl and run like hell, or lay for that sidewinder back of a rifle.

The first didn't encourage any great amount of hope, and just letting the other kind of squiggle through your noggin was enough to bring on the goddamn cholly morbus.

He took another gurgling swig.

Yet in spite of the shakes he kept turning it over. He might not have too much to be proud of but he certain sure couldn't just fold up and fade after giving out that he stood ready to take care of her.

The longer he considered, the stickier it looked.

He felt like banging his brains against a wall. The bottle didn't help, nor any notion he came up with. There wasn't nothing going to move that son of a bitch but a bullet!

★ ★ ★

Two days dragged past with no solution to his dilemma. The only sensible course was to get on his gray mule and get to hell out of this, but something stronger than sense kept him fuming and fretting and every time he started off to catch up his saddle he wound up throwing it down in disgust.

McCready, who stood to lose a good two-thirds of the mushrooming profits he'd expected to take out of this gold-plated deal, went about his skulduggeries back-slapping and laughing in the best good humor. If he was worried you'd never have guessed it to see him touring the camp or grinning and kidding with Rice and Tex Rickard. He hadn't been able so far to get a firm statement from Rickard as to whether or not he was going to move over here. He had bought two prime lots and brought in a contractor to figure out building costs but that was all anybody knew for sure.

Yet bigwigs were coming in now on every coach, some from as far away as Tonopah and Bullfrog. There was even a contingent come over from Ballarat, two gents from Choride and half a dozen from Cave Springs and Spangler. Nor were Rice,

Rickard and Knickerbocker the only ones who had quit the plush life of Goldfield to see what Salvation might have to offer.

High-stepping Nat Goodwin and Riley Grannan, the big plunger, had told McCready yesterday they were fixing to pull up stakes and throw in with him. Upward of twelve hundred people were on hand now, each of them trying to get the best of someone else. Town lots along the camp's busy street had tripled in value and McCready this morning had sold one for two thousand. A dozen heavy ore wagons, brand spanking new, with Salvation Mine painted across their high-wheeled sides, were parked at the head of the street waiting for the teams of mules the fat man was said to have sent for, and he was down at the mercantile five or six times a day pestering the clerks for news of his pumps.

There was talk of a telegraph line coming in and already application had been made for a post office. Only one piece of ugliness disturbed the lively picture of expectant prosperity: four of the Roman Five crew yesterday had engaged in a rumpus that had just about wrecked Alfred Caddy's Pink Elephant, breaking chairs and tables, smashing the mirrors, becoming a fist-swinging free-for-all before

Darling and his deputies had managed to put a stop to it.

Nobody knew what had set the pot boiling but Oberbit saw it as a straw in the wind, something instigated to remind them of what could happen if things didn't go the way Weminuche wanted.

McCready, if it bothered him at all, was not sufficiently put out of countenance to allow any sign of it to show. Pushed by some of the more civic-minded claim owners he did, as mayor, authorize the hiring of three extra deputies. But those available to accept such commissions were not, in Oberbit's opinion, like to be of much help if Clee's hard-nosed punchers really took to the warpath.

Micaela had him fighting his hat. He couldn't think what had got into her. Ever since Johnston had told the lawyer to skin his own rabbits she'd been hard to get into a conversation except in the company of the rusty-faced Darling or McCready himself. Even then she appeared considerably withdrawn, cool to the point of brusqueness. No telling what lies she'd been fed by that swindler.

In disgust and silently cursing them all, Oberbit had cinched up his mule and gone off to a high point overlooking the road to await Weminuche with the preacher and license he had said he'd fetch back.

A cool breeze was lifting, pulling whines of sound from the rattling brush.

Unless McCready could someway dispose of Micaela's claims before that walloper sashayed into camp he could look to get shoved right out in the cold — not that Johnston would shed any tears!

He hadn't come into this to benefit McCready. Only reason he'd ever come out here at all was he'd been pretty desperate to get hold of a stake, something that would keep a feller's wishbone from rupturing his belly till he could turn up another Silver King or Bull Weevil.

Way it looked now he probably wasn't ever going to.

Listening to the wind, he felt more deviled than he had back at Tombstone. This whole situation appeared ready to collapse. McCready, anyway, could dig for the tules — pick up what he'd garnered and head for new pastures. But the girl . . . she stood to be caught in the rubble, and Johnston right with her. Unless he cut loose of these quixotic notions.

Why should he stick his neck out to save her? She was between a forked stick that was studded with thorns, on one end

Weminuche, like a stick of capped dynamite; McCready on the other with his sharp shyster's tricks and the authority of the courts.

He watched the fat man pussyfoot through his mind again. It went against all reason to think a fat hog like him would ever stand up to pressure. Sure he'd faced Clee, but that was when he'd had everything going for him. What McCready had here was a busted flush and no sharpshooter Johnston had ever run into had ever called for showdown on that kind of hand.

No matter how cocky and imperturbable he looked, inside he had to be a mass of quivering jelly. The guy was putting on an act, trying to run a bluff, hoping to up the ante and get off with the pot before Weminuche could get back to stop him. Why else would he be so thick with Rice and Rickard, and this new fellow, Gannon?

Johnston thought again of those ore wagons conspicuously parked at the head of the street, and of the way McCready had been pestering the mercantile for news of the pumps he knew had never been ordered.

Yep — that was it. He was out to unload the whole blasted camp if he had his way, probably.

Like enough the bugger was packed right now, every last nickel stuffed into his pockets and a saddled brone waiting, ready to bolt with the whole kit and boodle — just playing for time to close this last deal and be off like white lightning before Weminuche got wind of what was up!

So look at this sensible, Oberbit decided. *There* was his stake. Let McCready fleece these promoters, figure he was clever, then shove a gun in his gut and take over.

It was the chance of a lifetime, no doubt about it.

XXX

With twin furrows of concentration between the glare-scrinched scowl of half shut stare, Johnston pulled himself into the saddle and nudged the floppy-eared mule into a drag-footed shuffle. Vaguely headed in the direction of camp, the bean-munching Tallow Eye, largely left to his own inclination, leisurely drifted among the clumps of mesquite as though scarcely caring whether school kept or not.

Oberbit, too wound up to notice, was gingerly examining the headful of thoughts unleashed in the wake of his bold conception. He was — if the strict truth be known — a little surprised at himself, the shadier didos in his past holding no suggestion of such reckless capability. He felt jumpy, too, his stomach uneasily filled with growls, yet withal strangely tickled at the drop-jawed prospect of McCready's consternation.

Intently scanning the proposal from a dozen different angles he turned up nothing which appeared unavoidably to threaten the probability of success. The fat man might have a sharp eye on Sammy but trouble from Johnston, *this* kind of trouble, was the last thing he'd look for.

Sure, he'd been a mite riled when Oberbit had told him of recording all the claims in the name of Micaela, but nothing approaching the rage a man would look for. Oberbit suspected that, secretly, he'd even probably been grimly pleased since everything held in Micaela's name was his to dispose of however he wanted, subject only, of course, to Micaela's signature which, however reluctant, he could count upon getting.

No, this ought to be easy as gutting a slut. And the finest part was it was all crooked money, acquired by means of dubious pretenses. Even having lost it at the point of a gun, McCready couldn't very well go running to the law!

At the rate he'd been selling stock in the mine and steadily inflating townsite lots that dude should have piled up plenty, not to mention sums extracted by threat of the land grant swindle from ranchers and railroads and whatever other sources his glib tongue had persuaded.

He wouldn't be the kind to put this hoard in a bank. Moving around as he'd been he'd want it handy always, ready and available in case, like now, he found it preferable to pull out. Why, he must have close to a couple hundred thousand!

Stimulated by this comfortable notion Oberbit's spirits leaped like soaring eagles. A stake like that would certainly keep a man the rest of his natural. There was only one obstacle that Johnston could see and this had to do with the matter of timing. Should he grab what he could straightaway and clear out, or wait, like McCready, in the hope that the fat shyster might successfully unload the rest of their holdings?

The smart thing, of course, was to strike and be gone before Weminuche got back to turn the tables.

But it was hard in these ballooning visions of prosperity to settle for any part of a loaf when with a bit more of waiting he might get the whole lot. Obviously this was what was holding McCready. He must believe he could get it or he'd not be fiddling around. A handful of hours must almost certainly see this finished; the old slicker would not risk being around this camp tomorrow.

Johnston narrowed his eyes as another hitch abruptly sidled into view: how to keep track of that shifty damned dude!

Might take some doing without he

camped on the walloper's shirttail. You couldn't follow the old bastard around like a dog . . . seemed a mighty poor time to be prodding up suspicions.

Suddenly Oberbit smiled.

There was a chance he might not have to. Any con artist slippery as Dan McCready would scarcely be courting disaster as he was without having looked to his getaway. He'd have his saddlebags packed and a horse cached out someplace.

Find the horse and you had your rabbit.

Night had shrugged into its sable coat by the time Tallow Eye fetched Johnston into camp. The street seemed inordinately ablaze with light; it seemed noisier, too, with a heavier crush of traffic than it usually had at this early hour. Everywhere Johnston looked there were knots of gesticulating, excitedly talking men. He felt his guts tighten up, glimpsed a glint of metal and swung out of the saddle to catch hold of Sammy. "What the hell's goin' on?"

"Ain't you heard?" Darling snorted. "You must be about as deef as Aunt Minnie Majors! One of them pick swingers not two hours ago busted into a vein of blue quartz damn near two foot wide!"

Johnston stared, mouth agape.

"You — you mean one of them fools I put to diggin' a hoist hole?"

"No." Sammy grinned like it tickled him. "One of them claim owners down in the gulch. Makes Dan's samples look like poor relations. That feller Gannon's already offered a hundred thousand dollars fer it — an' been turned down!"

XXXI

The new marshal shoved off, tin star a-twinkle with the reflections of torches and door-hung lanterns, swiftly engulfed in the restless surge of perambulating humanity excitedly in motion between one or another of the camp's six saloons.

Even if what Sammy'd said was all true it didn't have to mean a strike had been made; and, granting one had, Oberbit couldn't think it would alter McCready's intentions. For there was still Weminuche and his threat to come back with a preacher and marry the source of McCready's golden eggs. There wasn't the least doubt he'd demand an accounting, force McCready to disgorge or shoot him.

The fat man was through, no two ways about that. He was done the minute Weminuche hit camp. Just the same, it sure did shake a man up to think all of this while he might have been sitting on top enough gold to kick off a rush that didn't have to be staged. That fat slob of a dude must be feeling meaner than a new-sheared sheep unless this was something he had set up himself — which he damn well might have at that, Johnston thought.

It wasn't figured to hurt his prospects with Rickard and the rest of them out-of-town moguls he had on his string. Might be all that was needed to set fat Dan on the road to greener pastures.

Back on his mule Johnston took a hard look across the crowded street without sighting his quarry. His stomach was beginning to bid for his attention, but his mind was too filled with greater urgencies to work up any sweat over a missed meal or two.

He rode around for a while, up one side and down the other, trying to fit himself into the fat man's shoes, trying to think as a feller might imagine McCready would with all these ifs hanging over him. Unless the lawyer aimed to sell out for peanuts he would have to stay where the action was. Oberbit made inquiries and turned his mule in the direction of the lake bed and the glare of light being raised about the site of this latest discovery.

There was quite a mob around the claim but no sign of the man Oberbit was hunting. Generous samples were being passed around and Johnston, getting hold of one, had to admit it looked the real thing. He looked the crowd over for another several minutes without seeing any of that bunch from Goldfield. With tightening lips he headed back uptown.

Be a hell of a note if that two-legged snake had already cut himself loose and departed!

He went by the girl's tent and found it empty. In a kind of a panic he got back on his mule and was trying to dig up some other likely place when a man came around the tent's far side. Johnston lifted his voice. "You seen McCready?"

The man's head twitched around. Their eyes met and locked. Ossie Hampton said, "Try the Hardrock House," and set off toward the gulch, leaving Johnston staring after him, sudden prey to a disquiet he could not pin down.

Jerking Tallow Eye out of his half asleep trance, Oberbit swung the mule's nose toward the camp's one hotel, a garishly elegant structure only recently completed for formal opening today under the auspices of its builder, H. W. Knickerbocker, the oracular gospel-shouter from Goldfield.

What, Johnston couldn't help wondering, was the burly ex-teamster doing around Micaela's tent or, far as that went,

252

the other unlikely places he had lately been running into him?

He forgot about Hampton when he got to the hotel and, peering through a window, discovered McCready dining with Rickard, Gannon and George Graham Rice. What Oberbit found particularly significant was the presence there also of Micaela Peralta. He didn't reckon McCready would have bothered to fetch her without the smell of success was about to crown his efforts.

It was time, he decided, to hunt for that horse.

Didn't seem like McCready was at all apt to figure on returning to his headquarters at the townsite shack. Be too much of a giveaway to be seen departing from that vicinity, and the same went double for where he was now. It would look too suspicious for him to be seen signing papers with that bunch of plungers, then get on a horse and take off at this hour. Them moguls wouldn't like it, for one thing.

Yet he'd want the horse handy on account of Weminuche.

In trying to come up with the likeliest spot for hiding it something else occurred to Oberbit in connection with this projected departure. This was a hard cash country distrustful of paper.

Even with diligence McCready would find it anything but easy to convert his whole stake into the conveniency of currency. There was bound to be some left in silver and gold which made for bulk and was harder to manage. Since he could not leave a horse with a box or a satchel tied back of the saddle without arousing curiosity he must be on the horns of a considerable dilemma.

What *would* he do?

Hide it, of course, till he was ready to pick it up. In the townsite shack? That didn't seem likely. Too available to thieves. He would want it stashed where he'd have some kind of check on its safety.

Johnston grinned.

There was just one place in this entire camp continually under scrutiny of guards and guns. The closed-up tunnel of the Salvation Mine.

Now these precautions began to make sense.

It was no longer necessary to locate the horse. All a man had to do was keep that tunnel shack in sight, Johnston thought — and then remembered something else. If he jumped McCready there he'd have the guard, too, to contend with.

Better let Dapper Dan take off with his

loot, get a fix, give him a lead and then swing around to cut in ahead of him.

On the west rim overlooking the lake bed Oberbit pulled up and got off his mule at about the place where — it seemed ages ago — Weminuche's outfit had clandestinely met with whoever from Jubal Clee's Roman Five had left his tracks in the mud of the arroyo.

Johnston would like to have got nearer but couldn't very well take up a post in Clee's yard and the whole damned lake bed was staked out solid, stippled with tents and claim shacks, half a hundred campfires attesting to the presence of men who put no trust in neighbors.

Johnston's scrinched-up eyes held an uneasy scowl.

The new strike had been made less than two hundred feet below the mouth of the old Salvation tunnel and there was still a mort of lanterns bobbing around in that vicinity. The whole front of McCready's tunnel shack was clearly visible even from here. While he could not locate the guard — even be sure if the door stood closed or open — Oberbit could see plain enough how this unexpected showcase effect might well make a man peer again at his holecard.

A lot would depend on how much McCready'd stashed there, but with all of this light and commotion around it seemed reasonable the man would be forced to improvise, perhaps make other arrangements to get hold of whatever he'd cached there. Rattled enough he might even cut loose and go off without it!

Oberbit, licking dry lips, thought awhile about that. The paper portion of his loot McCready probably had on him. Johnston was no hog. There'd be a guard around someplace, but he could probably go over there and, guard disposed of, even come out with a box or a satchel without stirring up any great amount of interest; anyone noticing would suppose he was on some errand for the fat man.

Oberbit was tempted, though half his satisfaction lay in taking it off McCready. While less anxious for satisfaction than he was to get hold of a stake, the big reason he didn't settle for what could be got at handily was an unrecognized something concerned with Micaela. This he managed to rationalize by a process too intricate to unravel here.

Reminded of the way he'd been used throughout by that fat tub of lard in the elegant derby, Johnston told himself anyone could be maneuvered if given the right set of circumstances, and set out to prove it in the quickest way possible.

Reining Tallow Eye around with a boot in the short ribs he propelled him into the Roman Five yard and set up a shout that could have woken the dead. Men came running from every direction, most of them armed, some with rifles and scowls. Without giving them time to understand this commotion he demanded to see Clee, "and hurry it up!"

Someone fetched the old man onto the gallery.

"Weminuche wants your crew fetched to camp," Johnston said like Moses handing down the tablets.

The rancher looked him over. "How come he sent you? Last I heard you was working —"

"Does a man have to be a goddamn fool *all* his life?"

"But Bill said —"

"He says somethin' else now. I'm not too dumb to know a good thing when it's pointed out to me. I'm lookin' after myself an' you better believe it!"

Clee curled his lip. "All right. What's he want?"

"He wants your crew to get set to take

over the whole east end of that street. He's goin' to put McCready on the run an' take over. McCready's in the Hardrock House with them bigwigs from Goldfield. I'll pull the slob outa there. He'll likely grab himself a hitch. Bill's idea is he'll head for the mine; that's where he'll be waitin' — see? Soon's McCready's lit out Bill wants you to take that hotel plumb apart. Same kinda job you did in the Pink Elephant."

Clee said, grinning, "All right, boys. Get your horses."

When the cavalcade arrived in clear view of the hotel Johnston drew rein and said, "You fellas take up stations where he'll have no trouble seein' you but like you're expectin' him to tear off east. Once he gits goin' you can send a few slugs whistlin' over his head." He waved them away. "I'll wait till you git set."

There were three saddle horses and a rig with matched bays parked along the hitch rail flanking the hotel's veranda. Oberbit watched while the Roman Fives dropped out of their hulls and got the stage set for his big production, taking up posts at the corners of buildings, lounging in doorholes, hands hooked in shell belts, one guy with a rifle hunkering back of a horse trough.

He guessed it would look pretty convincing to McCready.

Leaving Tallow Eye on dropped reins by the tie rail he started up the steps. Someone half obscured in the shadows of the veranda appeared to be furtively peering through the window but drew back as he approached, dropping off the ends of the boards. Kind of looked to Oberbit like that feller Hampton but he was too fastened into the part he was playing to give any great amount of thought to it then.

Throwing open the door he crossed the carpeted lobby, stomped into the dining room and stopped by the table where the fat man sat smoking over coffee with the big three from Goldfield. "Who's this?" Rickard said, wrinkling up his nose as if the smell of Johnston offended him.

McCready said around his ten cent cigar, "Feller I hired t—"

"Where's the girl?" Johnston growled.

McCready fingered his chins and took a deep breath. "Ah . . . excuse me, gentlemen." He smiled, getting up, and maneuvered Johnston off into a corner out of earshot. "What the hell ails you, busting in here like this!"

"Where's Micaela?"

The fat man, weighing tone and look,

allowed most probably she'd gone to her tent. "Hardly ate any supper," he grumbled irritably. "Left" — he dug out his gold engraved watch — "about ten minutes ago," he said, peering. "Soon as she signed the papers —"

"Then you better git hold of her an' light out a-runnin'." In a sepulchral voice Oberbit told him, "Weminuche's in town. He's got that bunch from Roman Five —"

McCready shoved past looking like a shot rabbit and plunged from the room like he couldn't get out quick enough.

Johnston, grinning through his scraggle of beard stubble, winked at Rickard and the other dropped jaws astonishedly staring, sauntered into the lobby and, lifting the pistol from the top of his trousers, stood, head canted, staring at the ceiling until an outside racket of shouts and hoofbeats, shots and wheel sound, told him the fat man had taken the bait.

Pushing open the door with the barrel of his gun he stepped onto the veranda and peered through a pattern of dust-fogged shadows.

No longer expecting the man to make for the mine, he was not surprised to see him pass the gulch entrance, though he was somewhat startled when McCready swung the team in amongst the clutter of first-arrival tents that from here obscured the townsite shack which for all these days had been the swindler's headquarters.

Johnston, stifling a curse, jumped the veranda to hit the ground running, piled aboard the nearest horse and threw in the steel.

He found the rig and matched bays standing before Micaela's tent, out of which came a gabble of furious voices.

As Johnston flung from the saddle McCready burst out of the tent with a satchel under one arm, trying fiercely with the other to get loose of the girl.

At this precise moment Ossie Hampton, the ex-teamster, barreled out of the shadows behind the glint of a pistol, yelling, "Stop right there, all of you! Put that bag down, McCready — you're under arrest!"

Muzzle flame winked from the fat man's middle. Micaela screamed. Oberbit, diving, crashed into Darling, felt the legs swept from under him and jackknifed into a rolling scramble of flying fists. A knee fetched up suddenly found its mark and, as Sammy fell back in a gurgle of anguish, Johnston slapped him a couple back of an ear with a fist and, pulling clear, groped around in a panic, trying to locate his pistol.

McCready, clouting the girl away from him, made a lunge for the buckboard, caught hold of a wheel, lifted a foot toward the step and, bent over that way, stiffened into rigidity. Oberbit, following the bulge of his stare past the girl scrabbling around gathering sheaves of spilled banknotes, found Weminuche standing like a rip in the picture. One hand held a cheekstrap, the other was fisted around the tilt of a six-shooter.

McCready licked dry lips, began to shake like a dog in a blue norther. "Look," he gulped, "you'll get no argument from me. You can have the whole lot . . ."

"You bet." Weminuche's contempt came across like a smell. He said, "I'll have it anyhow," and dropped the fat man in his tracks, gun swiveling to show its horrid snout to Oberbit.

"So long, sucker!"

In the powderflash Johnston came lunging erect in frantic reaction. The crash of the report racketed over the flats. Weminuche's eyes in that twisted face clawed around in mingled shock and astonishment to fix in bitter glaze on the caught-up gun held in both the girl's hands. He staggered back half a step trying to brace himself against a wall that wasn't there, suddenly collapsing like the fall of a house of cards.

★ ★ ★

Oberbit looked a long while at the girl, watching her strip McCready's pockets, digging inside his shirt to pull out the crammed money belt, buckling it around her.

He got into the buckboard looking gauntly used up as something yanked through a knothole; he slumped corpse-like in silence while Micaela went past the tent and came back bent over the weight of the satchel.

Johnston sighed like Atlas holding up the whole world. Looked again at the eyes that were searching his face. "Climb in," he grunted, moving over to make room.

He took the satchel she handed up and reverently nudged it under the seat, then shoved out a fist and pulled her aboard. "Where to?" he grumbled, picking up the reins.

"I guess you know I wasn't raised in a convent?"

"Yeah," he said like it took all his breath. "I don't reckon you was christened Peralta, either."

She said, "Nothing so grand. I was a bar girl at Manuelito's when McCready hired me to take up that name."

"Well, at least," Oberbit told her, "you can live like one now."

"I intend to," she answered as he slapped the matched pair with a swing of the rein ends. "Whereabouts are we going?"

"From here on out you can leave that to me. First place, I reckon, will be in front of a preacher. You just ain't geared to traipse around alone."